STAMPEDE!

A new sound fell on their ears—a sullen rumble, swelling to the crescendo of thunder. Davy twisted in the saddle and his breath choked off in his throat. Not from the smoke or the heat, but from the scores of huge humped brutes pounding in their wake. Scores of shaggy buffalo, living steam engines capable of bowling over and then trampling any living thing under their driving hooves.

The herd, terrified by the inferno, was rushing to escape searing death. Eyes dilated, nostrils distended, they stampeded in a compact mass, reducing the grass to pulverized bits. As Davy looked on, a deer blindly bolted in their path. It was a doe, as terror-stricken as the bison. The poor creature vented a plaintive wavering bleat before vanishing under the brown tide.

Davy could have sworn that he heard the crunch of her bones. Spurring on the sorrel, he yelled at Becky, "Ride, girl! Ride!"

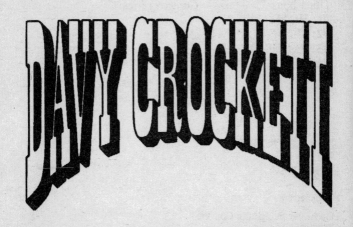

DAVY CROCKETT

COMANCHE COUNTRY

DAVID THOMPSON

LEISURE BOOKS NEW YORK CITY

To Judy, Joshua, and Shane

A LEISURE BOOK®

February 1998

Published by

Dorchester Publishing Co., Inc.
276 Fifth Avenue
New York, NY 10001

ISBN 0-8439-4356-4

Printed in the United States of America.

COMANCHE COUNTRY

Chapter One

"Is something on fire?"

Davy Crockett tilted his head back and sniffed. For the past hour, as his weary horse plodded eastward, he had been lost in thought. Instead of staying alert, as he should, he had been recollecting the series of events that explained why he was deep in the dark heart of the vast prairie and not safe and snug in his cabin in Tennessee.

Decisions were to blame. Bad decisions. *His* decisions. He was the one who had hankered to go on a gallivant. He was the one whose wanderlust was forever spurring him to see what lay over the next horizon. And he was the one who had persuaded his best friend to tag along in the belief they would be gone only a short while.

To be fair, Davy had not planned to wind up at the Great Lakes. Or, later, to clash with the Sioux and a band of vicious slavers. It had been his notion, though, to canoe down the broad Mississippi to St. Louis, cutting weeks off their return travel time. He was also to blame for dragging his friend off across the plain to find out why a solitary family in a single wagon had crossed the river and gone off across the grassland by themselves.

For once, Davy's curiosity had put him in the right place at the right time. He had been on hand to help the family when they were beset by treacherous whites and bloodthirsty Pawnees. He had saved the mother and her child, but could not prevent the loss of her man or their wagon and belongings.

It was the youngster, Becky, who had just asked the question that now made Davy aware of an acrid scent in the air. "That's smoke, all right," he confirmed.

"Way out here in the middle of nowhere?" the girl said. "Who could it be?"

The brawny Irishman wondered the same thing. Few whites roamed the shimmering sea of grass. Indians were another matter, and many of them were hostile to whites. He fingered Liz, his rifle, and rose in the stirrups to scan the prairie in all directions. The wind was blowing from the northeast for a change, but in that direction lay more of what they had been seeing for the past two days—namely, empty plain. "Mighty peculiar," he noted.

Flavius Harris, Davy's boon companion, lifted his moon face and scowled. Like Crockett, he wore buckskins and high moccasins. Also like Davy, he wore a powder horn and ammo pouch crisscrossing his chest, and a possibles bag rested under his left arm. But where his fellow Tennessean's frame was hard and muscular, Flavius was portly. Not soft, or weak, or flabby. Just stout through the middle, like a wild boar.

"I don't care who's out there," Flavius said curtly. "I vote we fight shy of them and keep on going." His worst fear was that a new crisis would arise. After weeks of grueling travel, of one narrow escape after another, he yearned to reach Tennessee. How he missed home! How he missed the simple pleasures he had always taken for granted! Things like gorging on tasty vittles, guzzling ale at his favorite tavern, coon hunting with his hounds. Oh. And his wife, Matilda, of course.

"I agree, pard," Davy said.

Flavius cocked his head. "You do?" Usually, the Irishman wanted to do the exact opposite of whatever Flavius felt was best. And usually, they wound up in a hornet's nest of trouble as a result.

Davy nodded. He had no desire to tempt fate and possibly put the girl and her mother in danger. They had been through so much already. Clucking to his sorrel, he rode on. Then Heather Dugan spoke.

"Hold up, you two. Shouldn't we investigate? What if white men are close by? Maybe they have supplies they can spare. Food they can give us."

None of them craved a piping hot meal with buttered bread and fresh coffee more than Flavius. He was tired of going hungry most of each day, tired of rabbit stew and fried snake for supper. But he quickly answered before his partner, saying, "We shouldn't go off half-cocked, ma'am. What if it's more Pawnees or other hostiles?" He shook his head. "No, I reckon it's a heap safer if we go about our own business."

Davy suddenly slowed. Tendrils of smoke had appeared on the horizon. Not one or two, as there would be if campfires were the cause. No, he counted a dozen spiraling strands that climbed to the clouds. Rather than the customary chalky white or wispy gray of most campfires, these were dark and sinuous, twisting snakes that seemed alive and ominous. "What the devil?" he blurted.

The acrid scent had grown stronger. A gust of wind brought with it invisible waves of heat, like the warm air that fanned Flavius whenever he opened the oven to check on his wife's pies and sweetcakes.

"It's a fire," little Becky said.

That it was, and the sight sent an icy chill down Davy Crockett's spine. He recalled the tale his Sioux friends had told him, about the summer a fire roared down without warning on their village. Half a dozen people had died, scores of horses had perished, and most of the lodges had been reduced to ashes.

"An awful big fire," Flavius amended. As near as he could tell, its front stretched over a mile long.

Davy applied his heels to the sorrel. "Let's not dawdle," he hollered. By holding to a gallop for a spell, they could outflank the blaze and travel on in safety. Or so he assumed until more tendrils materialized directly to the east. Figuring there must be a gap somewhere, he kept on riding. But the tendrils soon became thick columns, and the sky filled with what looked like a roiling black thunderhead.

"Goodness gracious!" Heather exclaimed. "It has us cut off." She ran a hand through her mane of luxurious blonde hair. Her dress clung to her full figure, the hem hiked up around her knees. She was a striking figure of a woman, a fact both Davy and Flavius were all too conscious of, particularly during the lonely hours late each night.

"Not quite," Davy said, and instantly reined to the south. He intended to parallel the fire until a break appeared. But the farther they went, the more apparent it became that the fire was much more extensive than he had imagined.

"The whole prairie is in flame," Becky commented. She had the black hair of her father, and frank blue eyes. Showing no panic, she asked calmly, "What do we do, Mr. Crockett? How do we reach the river now?"

Reaching the Mississippi was the least of their worries. Davy saw red and orange teeth spike out of the grass, devouring it greedily. Another warm gust warned him of a new development. "The wind shifted. It's blowing right at us."

"I don't like this," Flavius said nervously. "Let's hike our tails and skedaddle."

Added incentive came in the form of crackling and hissing that rapidly grew louder. The fingers of flame were now broadswords, cutting through the high grass like a scythe.

Davy motioned at Becky and Heather, shouting, "If you value your hides, ride like hell!"

The four horses were spurred into a pell-mell gallop. Davy deliberately stayed close to the girl. Her mare was a spunky critter, but it lacked the stamina of his sorrel and the other animals. Over his shoulder he fastened an eye on the swiftly advancing sheet of fire.

All that hissing reminded him of the time he had tossed a rock into a snake den. The crackling was louder than the racket caused by a herd of spooked elk making off through dense timber. And the heat had climbed so much, his face broke out in beads of sweat.

It became more uncomfortable by the moment. As impossible as it was to conceive, the fire was actually gaining. A yelp from Heather drew Davy's attention ahead, where another line of flame had flared. Now they were hemmed in on *three* sides. "To the southwest," he bawled, jabbing a finger.

Flavius jerked on the reins of his dun. His initial fear had worn off, to be replaced by rising anger. Just when his fondest wish had finally come true, when they were on their way home at long, long last, *this* had to happen. How could Providence be so cruel? What had he done to deserve to suffer so? Bending low over the dun, he lashed it so it would catch up with Heather Dugan.

The next moment, something streaked past on the right. Then on the left. Lithe figures, bounding high with every leap. Davy realized they were antelope, the kind some frontiersmen had taken to calling pronghorns on account of the unique short, broad horns they sported. The males had black bands from their eyes down to their nostrils, and black patches on their necks. The females usually did not have horns, and the does were slightly smaller than the bucks.

They were the fastest animals Davy had ever laid eyes on. Making bounds of more than twenty feet, they flew by him moving twice as fast as the sorrel. Most had their mouths open—not from fatigue, but to breathe more easily at full

11

speed. The white hairs on their rumps, longer than their other body hair, stood erect, giving the illusion that their backsides were twice as big as they truly were.

The Sioux had told Davy that in the summer, pronghorns congregated by sexes. The younger males formed bachelor herds, the older ones established territories, while the does and fawns roamed in small groups of a dozen or so. Yet here Davy saw bucks and does and fawns mixed. Fright had banded them together in stark flight.

Davy's coonskin cap was jiggling. He clamped it down again, then caught a whiff of smoke so potent that he broke into a coughing fit. The air overhead was becoming choked with the stuff. It stung his eyes, creating tears. He had to blink to clear them.

"We'll never make it!" the mother wailed. She was coughing, too, and swatting in vain at a grayish veil that had descended.

Flavius angled his dun in closer, in case Heather needed help. She had earned his undying devotion by nursing him after he was shot, and he would do all in his power to see her safe to St. Louis. In his idle moments, he fancied that she cottoned to him as much as he did to her, and he felt twinges of regret that he was not single. Twinges he would never own up to, not even to Davy. Should Matilda get wind of it, she'd brain him with her rolling pin or whatever else was handy.

A new sound fell on their ears—a sullen rumble, swelling to the crescendo of thunder. Davy twisted in the saddle, and his breath choked off in his throat. Not from the smoke or the heat, but from the scores of huge humped brutes pounding in their wake. Scores of shaggy buffalo, living steam engines capable of bowling over and then trampling any living thing under their driving hooves.

A small herd, terrified by the inferno, was rushing to escape searing death. Eyes dilated, nostrils distended, they stampeded in a compact mass, reducing the grass to pulverized bits. As Davy looked on, a deer blindly bolted into their path. It was a doe, as terror-stricken as the bison. The poor creature vented a plaintive wavering bleat before vanishing under the brown tide.

Davy could have sworn that he heard the crunch of her bones. Spurring on the sorrel, he yelled at Becky, "Ride, girl! Ride!"

"I am!" she cried.

But despite her efforts, the mare was flagging. Davy gave it a few whacks with the muzzle of his rifle, which convinced it to redouble its efforts. They pulled to within a few yards of her mother and Flavius. Sixty feet in front of them vaulted more antelope. To the left, the fire angled in their direction. To their rear was the irresistible tide of sinew and horns. Only to their right, to the west, lay safety.

"Follow me!" Davy commanded, hauling on the reins. He slowed just enough to make sure the others complied, then slowed even more so Becky could draw abreast of the sorrel. They were now racing almost at a right angle to the herd, which bore down on them like a living avalanche.

The earsplitting drumming drowned out the chorus of the flames. Davy risked a glance and wished he hadn't. A formidable wall of huge heads and wicked curved horns rushed toward them. There would be no stopping those buffalo, no turning the leaders with a few shots or shouts. Nothing on God's green earth could stem that hairy mass until it had spent itself in exhaustion.

"Faster! Faster!" Davy urged. But he doubted anyone heard him, not over the bestial bedlam. Seventy yards separated the sorrel from the iron wall. Then sixty. Then fifty. Davy focused on the open plain beyond to the exclusion of all else.

"Mr. Crockett!"

The child's wail cut through the Irishman like a red-hot knife through wax. Davy whipped around and saw that the mare had tripped in a prairie dog burrow and gone down.

Rebecca Dugan had been thrown clear. She was on her knees, her arms upraised, her face lit by fervent appeal.

"Help me! Please!"

Flavius and Heather had not noticed. The only one who could save Becky was Davy, and he never hesitated. Bringing the sorrel to a sliding halt, he wheeled the big horse and sped toward the girl, who was rising. Out of the corner of an eye he glimpsed the foremost row of buffalo, now less than forty yards distant, the tips of their horns glinting dully in the sunlight that filtered through the smoke.

"Hurry!"

Becky stared at the onrushing herd and froze. Her face turned pale. Young she might be, but she was mature enough to foresee her impending doom. And it filled her with the same fear it would instill in a grown woman.

"Be ready to catch hold!" Davy shouted, but she was too paralyzed to obey. Holding his rifle and the reins in his left hand, he leaned as far down as he dared and extended his right arm. Becky was gaping at the buffaloes. She started to shift, and for a few moments he dreaded that she would bolt, sealing her death and possibly his.

The thunderous roar of hooves was near deafening. Davy could not see much of the herd since he was on the off side of the sorrel, but he could hear them, and it seemed as if the very air were being buffeted by invisible mallets. The brutes were so close. So very, terribly close.

The sorrel reached the child. In the blink of an eye Davy scooped the girl into his arm and straightened, wheeling the horse again as he rose. It was none too soon. The leading ranks of shaggy behemoths were twenty yards off. He jabbed his heels into the sorrel, which spurted forward as if shot from a catapult.

They had to get past the last of the buffalo on the west edge of the herd. Fairly flying, Davy glanced at the bristling array of black horn tips. Any of them could disembowel the sorrel with one swipe. The horse appreciated its peril, for it

tapped a reservoir of endurance it had never before demon-
strated and galloped the fastest it had ever gone.

A dank, sweaty scent rose from the herd. The grunts of
the bulls were punctuated by the bawling of cows and some
calves. These were fleeting impressions Davy had in the seconds before the sorrel galloped into the clear. The last bull
swung at the sorrel's flanks but missed.

Without a break in their collective rhythm, the buffaloes
surged southward, raising a cloud to mark their passage.

Davy put them out of his mind the instant they were no
longer a threat. Where a city-bred man might have quaked
at his close scrape with eternity, to Davy it was just another
incident in a routine day. It was part and parcel of life in the
wilderness, where a body never knew from one day to the
next if he would be alive to greet the new dawn.

Besides which, there was still the fire to contend with. The
flames formed a solid blazing sheet from north to south and
were being fanned westward by the prevailing wind. Davy
held the sorrel to a gallop, clutching Becky to his chest. She
clung to him, her eyes closed, trembling now and again. Her
mother and Flavius were a full hundred yards ahead.

It struck Davy as odd that Heather had not looked back
to check on her offspring. Heather Dugan was a devoted
mother. Normally, she hovered over Becky like a proverbial
hawk to ensure that the girl did not come to harm. Some
might say she overdid it, but her behavior was perfectly un-
derstandable once the facts were known.

Her beauty masked a soul that had suffered more than its
share of heartbreak. Her father had died when she was
young. Her mother remarried, but the stepfather, one of the
richest and most powerful men in St. Louis, turned out to be
a demented tyrant who insisted she live by his rules. When
she wed a man he did not approve of, the stepfather nursed
a hatred that ended in violence.

Heather's husband had decided to take her away, to move
back east. But he died in a freak mishap at work—or so

15

everyone believed until much later when the stepfather boasted that he'd had her husband murdered to keep them from leaving. But that was after Heather and a new beau had fled.

Heather, like many attractive women, always drew suitors like honey drew bears. She was lucky enough to fall in love a second time, to a man named Jonathan Hamlin. Together, they conspired to buy a wagon and supplies and strike out for the Oregon country. It had been their wagon tracks, and Becky's footprints, that so aroused Davy's concern he had trailed them to warn them of the ordeal they were letting themselves in for.

Unknown to Heather and Hamlin, Alexander Dugan, the stepfather, had learned what they were up to and had been in feverish pursuit. He caught them, too. Against her will, Heather was forced to head back toward St. Louis. But along the way, the group was beset by a war party of Pawnees. The Indians slaughtered everyone except the mother and daughter, who would have perished along with everyone else if not for Davy and Flavius.

Now here they were, fleeing for their lives, thwarted in their attempt to reach civilization by a wildfire. What started it was irrelevant. Maybe a lightning strike miles distant. Maybe coals from a campfire long extinguished. Who could say? All that mattered to Davy Crockett was survival.

The wind was dying down, a good omen. The Irishman slowed to spare the sorrel from exhaustion later on. He was about to open his mouth and yell for Flavius when Becky stirred and gazed fondly at him.

"Thanks for saving my life, Mr. Crockett."

"Consarn it, girl. How many times must I tell you to call me by my first name?" Davy patted her raven hair, then chuckled. "Saving damsels in distress comes naturally to us knights in shining armor. Haven't you ever heard tell of Ivan-hoe?"

Becky's face was blank. "Ivan-who?"

Davy let it drop. The child was too young to have heard of Sir Walter Scott, or the sensation Scott's stories had created on both sides of the Atlantic just a few short years before. Davy had never read any of them himself. He tended to treat books as he would the bubonic plague. They were an embarrassing reminder of the all-too-few years he had spent going to school, and how little he had managed to learn during those years. It was largely thanks to an aunt of his, an avid reader, that he knew about Scott and Ivanhoe.

"My mother says we can never thank you enough for all you've done for us," Rebecca said in her clipped, precise English.

"Shucks, we just happened to be in the right place at the right time," Davy responded. Or, as Flavius would have it, the wrong place at the right time.

It was strange, Davy mused, how life worked out sometimes. For weeks on end Flavius had insisted they quit the gallivant and light a shuck for home and hearth. If Davy had heeded him, if they had gone back sooner, odds were that Heather and her daughter would be dead, or, worse, under the iron thumb of Alexander Dugan.

A crackling noise signaled that the flames were gaining again, owing to the fickle wind. It gusted from the southeast now, the sheet of fire advancing in a solid wave of red and orange. He prodded the sorrel into full flight.

Just then the wind shifted once more. Blustery bursts pushed the conflagration in a wide arc that looped around the Tennessean and the child, threatening to cut them off. Becky cried out as flames more than six feet high swept toward them. Davy slanted to the right, seeking to avoid being encircled, but the persistent wind had a will of its own. Sizzling flames spread in a wide front, barring his path.

A narrow gap remained. Once it closed, they would be trapped. Davy cut the reins and barreled toward the opening. They were nearly there when the sorrel slowed, upset by the intense heat and the racket. Davy flailed his legs and pumped

17

his arm, but it did no good. The sorrel simply refused to brave the scorching tempest. In frustration, Davy slammed the stock of the rifle down.

Whinnying stridently, the sorrel plunged into the closing gap. Fire licked at them on both sides. Searing but brief agony lanced up Davy's legs. Another heartbeat, and they were ahead of the wildfire again, though by only a few yards.

Fingers of flame leaped high, slashing at the animal's hindquarters. It was enough to inspire the sorrel to put more distance between it and the fire. Gradually, bit by bit, they covered enough ground to be temporarily safe.

Davy wanted to let the sorrel rest, but it would be unwise. He held to a brisk pace for more than a quarter of a mile, until Heather Dugan turned, saw her daughter in his arms, and promptly drew rein. Flavius imitated her, his surprise equally apparent.

"What the dickens? Where'd her mare get to?"

The last Davy had seen of it, the horse was struggling to stand after snapping a leg in the prairie dog burrow. He had not witnessed the gruesome outcome, which was just as well. There had probably not been enough left of the mare to identify it as a horse. In reply, he shook his head.

"Damnation. That's a shame," Flavius said. It wasn't that he had grown fond of the animal. He was thinking that now it would take longer to reach St. Louis.

The mother kneed her bay alongside the sorrel. "Here. I'll take over," she offered, and switched Becky to her own saddle. Grime streaked Heather's features, and sooty black smears dirtied her hair and clothes. She was a far cry from the vision of beauty she customarily presented.

Davy studied the wildfire. The wind had blown the westernmost edge back in on itself, resulting in a backfire that had brought the writhing fiery serpent to a stop. On that front, at least. Far to the south and the north the plain still burned.

"What do we do next?" Heather asked.

Their choices were limited. Traveling due east was out of

the question. Even if the fire dwindled, hot pockets would persist for days. Swinging northward was likewise impractical. Since that was the compass point that had spawned the inferno, common sense told Davy that they would encounter nothing but scorched earth for countless miles. Their best bet, he figured, was to ride to the south. Eventually the flames would die out and they could continue to the Mississippi. So that was what he proposed.

"Fine by me," Flavius immediately remarked. "Let's get going." Any delay, however small, he resented. After weeks on end of wandering just for the sake of satisfying the Irishman's craving for adventure, his desire to see Tennessee again eclipsed all else.

The rest of the day was uneventful. They stayed away from the fire, and it obliged by not coming toward them. The prevailing breeze coaxed it steadily southward. By evening Davy could no longer see the leading border of blackened land, even when he stood in the stirrups. The flames had outdistanced them.

Camp was made for the night in a gully that sheltered them from the bracing air. Davy and Flavius took turns keeping watch. Heather insisted on taking a turn, but Davy let her sleep. She had lived through a virtual nightmare the past few days; she needed all the rest she could get.

First light found them in the saddle. Breakfast consisted of the last of their jerked venison. To quench their thirst, Davy collected dew by spreading out a blanket, then wringing it over their coffeepot. Most went to the horses. Without their mounts, their prospects of reaching St. Louis were slim.

The grass to the east had been charred to cinders. Hot spots were frequent. Noon came, and still they detected no sign of the end of the burnt belt. Davy was constantly on the alert. He did not say anything to the others, but he was worried. Every mile took them deeper into the grassland, deeper into the realm of the unknown, deeper into country teeming with hostile tribes and savage beasts.

Who knew what might happen?

Chapter Two

By the middle of the afternoon Flavius Harris wanted to scream. Every mile they covered without being able to turn east added to his irritation. Circumstance forced them to go farther and farther south, ever farther from where they had cached their canoes, ever farther from the river that was their link to St. Louis.

Never in his wildest dreams had Flavius imagined a fire could lay waste to so much land. Mile after mile lay black and blistered, smoke rising from sections that still smoldered. He began to fret that the fire had gone clear to Texas, that it would be a coon's age before he set foot on his homestead again, that by then Matilda would have thrown all his belongings into the trash heap and taken herself a new man.

Then things got worse. During the previous night the blustery winds had sent the flames to the southwest. Now Davy and the others were compelled to swing almost due west to go around, adding to the delay.

Flavius fidgeted and fumed. He made up his mind that if

Davy ever asked him to go traipsing off on another gallivant, he would shoot himself in the foot so he'd have a valid excuse to say no.

Along about three o'clock, Davy decided that enough was enough. He turned east. But as soon as the sorrel stepped onto the blackened shreds of grass, it acted up. Shying and nickering, it refused to go farther. Heather's mount would not even come close to the burnt area.

Flavius was overjoyed to discover that his animal was not bothered in the least by the acrid stink or the tendrils of smoke and soft hissing. He could, if he was so inclined, go on alone and wait at the Mississippi for the others to catch up. But he could not bring himself to abandon them. Also, the notion of being alone in the midst of the wilderness downright petrified him.

They continued westward. After another hour, they were able to forge to the south again. Davy considered it just their dumb luck that the wind, which usually issued from the northwest, had been blowing out of the north-northeast when the wildfire broke out.

Twilight caught them in the open, with no water nearby. While Flavius tethered the horses, Davy gathered grass, took the flint and steel from his possibles bag, and soon had a small fire going. Small, because at night the glow from a campfire could be seen from far off and he did not care to advertise their presence to any unsociable Indians who might be in the general vicinity.

Davy hunted for game for more than an hour but came up empty-handed. The fire had killed or driven off every last creature. There were no rabbits, no snakes, nothing. A few pieces of pemmican sufficed for supper.

A quiet night ended in a cold dawn. A little coffee was left, which Davy rationed to make it last longer. Flavius was as grumpy as a bear just out of hibernation, while Heather complained about needing a bath.

Only little Becky did not grouse. She greeted each of them

with a warm smile and kind words. They could take a lesson
from her—and from all youngsters, Davy reflected as he assumed the lead. Children naturally took setbacks in stride,
more so than adults, who were supposed to be more mature.

Toward the middle of the morning, Davy was lost in memory, recollecting the last time he had gone bear hunting with
his prized hounds. Of all life's pastimes, of all a man could
do, he most enjoyed taking his rifle and coon dogs and heading into the hills or the deep cane after bruins. An uncle with
a lick of education once called it his "abiding passion,"
which was as good a way as any of describing how he felt.

Davy made no bones about it. First and foremost, he was
a hunter. He always had been. Ever since he was knee-high
to a calf, roaming the timber and swampland with a gun in
hand thrilled him as nothing else could. Hunting was in his
blood, in his bones.

It had gotten him into no end of trouble when he was a
boy. All because he had the habit of treating himself to days
off from school so he could hunt. His brothers had covered
for him, telling the schoolmaster he was sickly. But one time
he overplayed his hand.

It happened that an older boy had taken to picking on him,
and pushing him, and doing what bullies generally do. So he
had lain in wait for the culprit in a patch of bushes. When
the bully came along, out Davy sprang to give him salt and
vinegar. He had clawed the boy's face all to a flitterjig, and
won the day.

But since the boy was bound to tell the schoolmaster, who
was partial to a hickory switch always propped in a corner
of the schoolhouse, Davy elected not to go to school the next
day. Or the next. Or the next. He had started to believe he
could go on deceiving both his folks and the schoolmaster
forever, when the latter played dirty—he wrote a letter to
Davy's father.

That did it. The wrath of the Almighty descended on the
Crockett cabin. Incited by a few horns of liquor, Davy's pa

23

warned him that if Davy did not go to school the next day, there would be hell to pay.

Any boy with a lick of sense would have gone. Davy knew that. He knew what was best. Which made it harder to explain exactly why he went against the grain. For the very next morning, as promised, there stood his pa, righteous wrath incarnate. "Off you go," his father commanded. And off Davy went—in the opposite direction.

His father snatched up a switch and gave chase. For more than a mile Davy held his own. Then he hid, and soon his father went huffing and puffing by, like a steam boiler about to burst.

Unwilling to go to school, and even more unwilling to be beaten, Davy took the only course he felt was open to him. He ran away from home, hiring on as a cattle drover on a drive to Virginia. For more than two years he made do as best he could, often with little more to his name than the clothes on his back and few coins in a poke. And all because he would rather hunt than learn his ABCs.

A snort by the sorrel brought Davy's idle musing to an end. Glancing up, he saw an enormous basin to his left and moved to the rim. Below was the same buffalo herd that had nearly trampled him to death. Or so he assumed, since there had been no trace of any other.

They were all dead.

Apparently, the herd had stampeded into the north end of the basin, down a gradual incline, and come to a stop. Probably, at the time, they had been well in front of the fire. Being tired and hungry, they had milled about, grazing.

Down there they could not see the wall of flame creeping closer, ever closer. From the evidence, the wildfire had raged right up to the north rim, then along the east edge and around to the south. The grassy slope had given the hungry flames access to the basin floor. Trapped, the bison had sought a way out, but only to the west was the prairie untouched, and the west side of the basin was a sheer wall more than ten feet high.

At its base, the fire caught them. They had scrambled madly to get out, their hooves leaving deep gouge marks in the dirt wall. No doubt many had been crushed in the press of heavy bodies. The thick, lush grass, so sweet to their taste, was the instrument of their destruction. Dry as tinder, the whole bottom of the basin had ignited, roasting the bison alive.

Davy looked down on a jumbled mass of burnt carcasses. Skulls and rib cages littered the ground. A few of the great beasts had not been entirely consumed. Charred patches of hide and rotting meat clung to darkened skeletons. The reek of burnt flesh was overpowering. Covering his mouth and nose with a hand, Davy rode off.

No one said anything. Becky averted her eyes. Heather showed no emotion. Flavius, though, lingered, searching for a carcass worth eating. As famished as he was, he would settle for a lump of partially cooked flesh. But none of that incinerated mass appeared appetizing enough. It was either too burnt or too putrid.

As Flavius nudged his horse on, he gazed skyward to note the position of the sun and spied large birds circling over-head. Buzzards. Not many, but that would soon change. Vultures had an uncanny knack for knowing when a feast was handy. He toyed with the idea of shooting one for supper, but he did not lift his rifle. Buzzard meat was the most god-awful any man ever ate.

The sun climbed to its zenith and commenced its descent. Flavius mopped his brow, commenting to no one in partic-ular, "This will learn me to buck my wife."

Becky faced him. She was riding behind her mother, her arms around Heather's waist. "How's that, Mr. Harris?" she politely asked.

"My missus warned me not to go on this trek," Flavius informed her. "She boxed my ear, and told me the only

25

reason I was going was to get out of work. There was this stump that needed pulling, and a field that needed plowing. And the chicken coop leaked something dreadful.''

"In other words," Heather said, "your wife knows you well.''

Flavius nodded. "She was as right as rain, ma'am. I hankered for some time to myself. Figured a short gallivant couldn't hurt none. So I packed my bag and cut out, Matilda giving me the evil eye from the doorway.''

"You must love her a lot.''

The statement so shocked Flavius that his mouth dropped open. No one had ever accused him of that before.

Heather grinned at him. "No need to act so surprised. You talk about her all the time, and no man would unless he was profoundly in love.''

"Love, is it?" Flavius countered. "I wish I'd known sooner. I wouldn't have been so upset all those times she walloped me on the noggin with her frying pan." He tapped a spot where she had hit him shortly before he left. "Maybe you have something there, though. If lumps are a sign of affection, then I'm up to my neck in romance.''

The mother grew somber. "Be thankful you have a woman who cares for you. Both of the men I loved are gone, and I doubt I'll be smitten by Cupid a third time.''

"You never know" was Flavius's philosophical reply. "A pretty woman like you is bound to attract more menfolk.''

"Oh, that's never been a problem," Heather conceded. "The trick is to attract the right kind of man. Drunks and women-beaters and the like, I can do without." She sighed loudly. "I used to think that true love was as common as sand on a beach, but now I know different. It's a treasure, as rare as precious gems, as pure as the finest gold. When a person finds it, they should hold on to it for all they are worth. Relish every moment of happiness, because we never know when fate will deprive us of it.''

Flavius opted to change the subject. "I've been meaning

to ask. With your stepfather gone, who takes over his business empire?''

''Not me, if that's what you're thinking. Alex had two sons who will likely fight for control. They're both chips off the old block, mean and spiteful and money-hungry.'' Heather stared eastward. ''Frankly, I doubt my stepfather even mentioned me in his will.''

''So what will you do? Leave St. Louis?''

''I have relatives in Philadelphia. The City of Brotherly Love, it's called. Sounds like a real nice place to raise a child. And at this point in my life, rearing Rebecca properly is more important than anything else. I want her to have a chance at the happiness that has eluded me.''

Becky patted her mother's shoulder. ''It doesn't matter where we live. Just so I'm with you.''

Davy Crockett had been listening with half an ear. Over a shoulder he remarked, ''My grandma used to say that when life is treating us poorly, the best medicine is some tincture of time.''

''Time heals all wounds. Is that it?'' Heather responded. ''I'm sorry, Davy. But there are some hurts that never heal, not if we live an eternity.''

That put an end to their conversation for a while. Davy paralleled the burnt expanse, marveling at how the ground continued to give off smoke so long after the fire had gone by. It was well past noon when a stiff breeze from the southeast heralded the appearance of a slate-gray cloud bank.

A storm front was moving in. It accounted for the drastic shifts in wind over the past twenty-four hours. And it gave Davy cause to smile. ''Look yonder,'' he said, pointing. ''That there's our salvation.'' The rain would extinguish the hot spots and render the burnt grassland safe.

Flavius whooped and swung his beaver hat in the air. ''Hallelujah, and pass the gravy! This coon's prayers have been answered! The next full moon, I'll be sitting in my rocking chair guzzling a jug of old man Spencer's corn whiskey."

"My mother says that drinking is bad for you, Mr. Harris," Becky mentioned.

"Maybe so, girl," Flavius said. "But some bad habits are worth the price. Whiskey puts zest in a man's veins."

"And tangles his brain in knots," Heather declared. "Hard liquor and shallow minds go hand in hand. My stepfather was a drinking man, and look at how he turned out."

"Don't blame the liquor," Flavius said. "He was one of those self-made gents, and they tend to worship their creator. Why, they get so high on themselves, they walk on clouds for sport."

Becky laughed merrily. "You sure have a colorful turn with words, Mr. Harris. I bet you'd make a dandy mayor or senator."

"Not me, child. That's my partner's bailiwick. He can talk a coon out of a tree with that velvet tongue of his."

Becky giggled. "Oh, he cannot!"

"Care to bet?" Flavius brought the dun up next to their mount. "Well, bend an ear. Once, about four years ago it was, Davy and me went coon hunting up to Franklyn County. Found us a likely spot and pitched camp. It was late evening when our hounds treed something and we went for a look-see. Bless me if they hadn't cornered a coon on their own. It was a whopper, girl, as big as two ordinary coons put together."

"Did you shoot it?"

"Weren't no need." Flavius lowered his voice as if confiding a secret. "You see, Davy walked up to that tree as pretty as you please and asked that coon to come on down without a fuss. Well, of course the coon declined. 'Leave while you can,' he said to us, 'or I'll jump down there and rip your innards out.'"

Becky's eyes narrowed. "How old do you think I am? Raccoons can't talk."

Flavius recoiled as if he had been slapped. "Would I lie you? No, they don't talk like we do. But they have a nguage all their own, grunts and snarls and growls that any vvy woodsman can translate." Warming to his topic, he sumed. "So there this uppity coon was, threatening to tear s and the hounds to pieces if we didn't scat. Davy looked at varmint right in the eye and said, 'Listen here, critter. m Davy Crockett, halfman, halfgator, the terror of the cane-rake and the best hunter who ever donned buckskin. I wres-e whirlwinds for fun and drink lakes dry when I'm thirsty. can shoot the wings off a fly at a hundred paces, and the ars off a jackrabbit at two hundred. So climb on down here nd be done with this chatter.'"

The girl was hooked. "What did the raccoon do?"

"What else could it do? 'You're Crockett?' it squealed, nd proceeded to shed its skin right there on the spot. Threw down to us, tail and all." Flavius nodded at the Irishman. Davy wears it as his hat."

"You're joshing," Becky said, but she laughed nonethe-ess.

Heather cast a critical eye at Harris and commented, "If ou tell tall tales like this when you're sober, I shudder to nink what you're capable of after a few drinks."

Davy was a dozen yards ahead, seeking a draw or gully which to take shelter from the impending storm. The cloud ank was much closer, the wind had gained in strength, and e scent of moisture hung heavy.

A promising cleft to the southwest broadened into a dry vash. The walls were steep, but plenty of breaks wide nough for a horse permitted Davy to reach the bottom with-ut difficulty.

Flavius and the others followed. The prospect of heading omeward had him in fine spirits, and he announced, "After ve're back in Tennessee, I think I'll hold a social. Invite veryone to a dance and barbecue."

"You?" Davy said. As long as he had known his friend,

Flavius had shunned frolics and the like, branding them as excuses for the biddy hens to gossip and nothing more. The truth was that Matilda loved to dance, and Flavius didn't. And Matilda always had her way. She would drag Flavius from the shadows and swirl him around until he was worn to a frazzle. Once, he had feigned a sprained ankle. But Matilda was too smart for him; she "accidentally" dropped a keg on his feet. Or tried to. Flavius jumped aside to save himself, and when Matilda accused him of shamming, he claimed a miraculous cure.

"Why not me?" Flavius rejoined. It would be so wonderful to be home, he could even put up with neighbors he disliked.

Becky had limped off up the wash, exploring the nooks and crannies. Davy saw, and hastened to catch up. "Better be careful," he advised. "Rattlesnakes like to hide under flat rocks like these." Nudging one for emphasis, he bent and turned it over. A small lizard scuttled between his legs, making him jump, and into a clump of brush. "Among other things," he added dryly.

Becky tittered. "It looks as if you're the one who should watch out," she joked. Limping toward a bend, she paused to lift several more rocks. "I like wild animals. Back home I had a cat that was run over by a carriage, and a frog I caught in a pond. He was real cute. I named him George, after President Washington. Every morning I went out and gathered bugs for him to eat." Her mouth curled down.

"Did you let him go when you left for the Oregon country?" Davy asked, guessing that was why she had become sad.

"No. George was murdered."

"Murdered?"

"By my grandfather. He never did like George, and always complained that George made too much racket." Becky bit her lower lip. "George croaked a lot, especially at night. I covered the washtub with a blanket, but it was no

30

se. My grandfather was still upset." Pausing, she put her
and close to her chest, palm up, as if she were holding
omething. "One day I went to feed him and George was
one. Mother helped me search for most of the morning."

"Did you find him?"

The girl absently nodded. "Stomped to a pulp in the
lower garden. Someone took him from the washtub, carried
im outside, and killed him." Closing her hand, she shivered.
'We never would have found him if not for my grandfa-
her's dog. It was Rufus who pulled George out of the flow-
rs, just as if he knew where George was."

Davy did not ask if she suspected anyone. There was no
need. They both knew who was to blame. "How did your
grandfather feel about cats?"

"Come to think of it, the same as he did about frogs."
Becky squared her slim shoulders. "But all that is water
under the bridge, as my mother keeps telling me. When we
get to Philadelphia, she promised I could have a puppy. I
can hardly wait."

Becky limped on, the Irishman unable to take his eyes off
her crippled leg. Yet another legacy of Alexander Dugan's
bile, a burden the innocent child must bear for the rest of
her life. Hatred, like tainted water, was a bitter poison that
had an effect on everyone who came into contact with it.

Out of the blue, Becky said, "I don't blame you for what
you did, Mr. Crockett. My grandfather was a bad man. He
deserved to be shot."

Davy was jolted. He did not think she knew. Unbidden, a
vivid remembrance washed over him. Of the Pawnee attack.
Of the confusion and bloodshed. Of Alexander Dugan's men
being slain in pitched battle, but not Dugan. Unscathed, Dugan had climbed onto a white stallion to escape. There had
been no one else to stop him, no one to prevent him from
terrorizing Heather anew, of making her life's—and
Becky's—miserable for all their born days.

As Davy's grandpa and pa had been so fond of saying,

"Always be sure you're right, then go ahead." So Davy had done what he thought was right. He had shot Dugan himself, and struggled to come to terms with his deed ever since. Killing game was one thing, killing people another, killing people in cold blood something else entirely. "I wish there had been some other way," he said sincerely.

"So do I," Becky said. "For all the bad my grandfather did, he did a lot of good, too. Most of the time he treated me kindly, and he was always giving me gifts. He also gave a lot of money to an orphanage."

"He did what?" Davy said, blanching.

"Every January, on his birthday. He grew up in one, and it was his way of repaying the nuns who had helped raise him. Or that's what he told me."

Evidently the old axiom about there being some good in the worst of men was true. Davy slowed, torn by the revelation. He would not sleep well that night, and for however many more it took to come to terms with what he had done.

A sharp cry from Becky snapped Davy out of his funk. She had disappeared beyond the bend. He hurried forward, leveling the rifle in case she had stumbled on a rattler or something worse. But she was fine, standing beside a pile of old bones and holding an odd object in her hands.

"What is this, Mr. Crockett?"

It was a helmet, but one unlike any Davy had ever seen. Fashioned of burnished bronze, it had downturned brims that curved sharply upward at each end to form pointed peaks. A high metal comb crowned it from end to end. Beside the bones was a cuirass and a long spear or lance. Perplexed, Davy leaned Liz against the side of the wash and picked up the spear, then realized he had been mistaken. "Tarnation! It's a pike. The Spaniards used them, ages ago."

A little farther up the wash were more bones and more armor. Davy counted four skulls in all. One had a jagged rent where a bludgeon had caved in the bone. Another had a hole in it such as an arrow might make. A third lay atop a nearly intact skeleton, sternum of which had clearly been transfixed by a lance that shattered a pair of ribs when it exited the body.

"What were they doing here?" Becky wondered.

"Exploring, I reckon." Davy had heard tales, as practically everyone had, of the early Spanish explorations in Florida and the regions north of Mexico. The Fountain of Youth. The Seven Cities of Gold. Stories every boy never tired of hearing. But for the life of him, he could not recollect what the soldiers had been called.

"They were conquistadores," Heather Dugan said, providing the answer. She was at the bend, with Flavius. Walking to the nearest pile, she leaned down to run a hand over the cuirass. "Perhaps advance scouts for Coronado."

"Who?" Flavius asked. The armor astonished him, but the bones unsettled him more. He did not like being around death. Whether long dead or recently slain, corpses and bones and such sparked a queasy feeling deep in his gut.

"Francisco Vásquez de Coronado. Didn't you study him in school? He wasted a good many years searching for cities of gold that don't exist." Heather moved the cuirass, revealing a rusted dagger. "I didn't know he came this far north."

A brisk blast of cold wind brought Davy's head up. In the excitement of the moment he had forgotten about the approaching storm. Swirling clouds spanned the sky from horizon to horizon. The scent of rain was intoxicating. They had gone without much water for so long that he was eager to drink to his heart's content. Even the horses would— A thought jarred him, and he spun. "Did you tether the horses?"

Flavius blinked. He had heard Becky's cry and rushed to investigate, forgetting to tie the reins so the animals could not stray off.

Davy pivoted and jogged off. Losing their mounts would be a catastrophe. But he was not overly worried. No thunder had pealed, no lightning flashed. And rain had yet to fall. Then he heard a distinct *crack* almost at his feet, and, looking down, he saw what appeared to be a large white marble. Another smacked to earth seconds later. More fell, in twos and threes. Suddenly it was a deluge, a downpour of egg-size hail.

Around the bend a horse whinnied in fright and hooves clattered on stone.

Chapter Three

It was like being pelted with a hundred rocks at once. Davy Crockett raised an arm over his face to ward off the barrage as he rounded the turn. Hail smashed against his head, against the back of his neck, against his shoulders. Searing pain made him flinch at many of the blows. He drew up short in consternation on seeing the rump of the sorrel go up and over the south wall. The other horses were already gone.

Frantic, Davy scrambled to the top of the wash, dirt and small stones sliding out from under him. He could not hear much of anything above the hammering roar. The hail was thudding to earth like grapeshot from a cannon. Reaching the rim on his hands and knees, he let an oath escape him. A white wall hemmed in the wash. So thick was the hail that visibility was limited to less than ten feet.

A faint screech pulled Davy back to the bottom. It had sounded like Becky. Flying to where he had left the others, he was dumbfounded to find they were gone. "Flavius!" he hollered. "Heather! Where are you?"

From up the wash a bellow galvanized Davy into motion. He had not gone far when a vague shape loomed on the right. It was Flavius, huddled over Heather, who in turn was hunched protectively over Becky. All three were under a small overhang. Erosion had scooped a hole out of the side, leaving barely enough space for the three of them to crowd in. Pressing in close, his back to the hail, Davy asked, "Is anyone hurt?"

"The girl panicked," Flavius reported. He didn't blame her. The blistering onslaught was enough to beat a grown man down. He had a score of bruises and welts, he was sure. If not for his thick beaver hat, he'd have a dozen lumps to go along with them. "She ran, and we had to catch her."

Davy had to strain to hear what his friend said. The wash resounded to the nonstop pounding. It was louder than the buffalo stampede had been, louder than the peal of church bells or the hullabaloo of a frolic in full swing. Becky, he saw, was shaking and shivering even though the temperature had not fallen drastically. "It shouldn't last long," he shouted.

But he was wrong. As if to spite him, Mother Nature threw a tantrum of awesome magnitude. For minutes on end the hail fell, covering the bottom of the wash and filling it inch by gradual inch. Ten, twelve, fifteen inches, and still the level rose. Just when it seemed the hail would go on forever, it abruptly stopped.

The sudden silence was in itself unnerving. Davy cautiously glanced up at the clouds, now darker than ever and moving more slowly. "It's safe," he said, and moved out from under the overhang. To the south a flash of lightning lit the sky, shattering the stillness. It preceded new gusts of wind, violent gusts that shrieked and moaned like a demon gone berserk.

"Let's mount up and ride," Flavius suggested. Soon it would rain, and if there was one thing he disliked more than being pummeled by heavy hail, it was being soaked to the skin by freezing rain. A person could become sickly that way. As his folks had impressed on him, the human body was not meant to be wet. Which was why the Harris children took only one bath a month.

"We can't," Davy said.

Heather divined the reason and gasped, "They're gone? How will we survive without them?"

"They won't stray far," Davy predicted. "We'll find them easily enough." But he was being unduly optimistic. The animals might not stop running until they reached the Gulf of Mexico. "Come on."

Wading through the fallen hail, they filed to a gap and through it onto the prairie. A magnificent yet eerie vista greeted them, a sea of white spreading as far as the eye could see. Not a solitary creature stirred anywhere. Not even a bird or insect.

"Where did our animals go?" Becky asked.

Davy was at a loss. The hail had obliterated every last trace of their tracks. He had a hunch the horses had gone south, but what if his hunch was wrong? Four lives depended on his judgment; he could ill afford mistakes. "We'll have to hunt for them."

A cold drop spattered Davy's cheek as he strode off. Another stung his cheek, his temple, his chin. The rain had begun, big cold drops, harbingers of worse to come. He debated going back to the overhang to wait out the storm, and those few seconds proved costly.

A rumble of thunder was muffled by a cloudburst. "Oh, no!" Heather wailed. She vainly sought to cover her head with her arms. The torrent utterly drenched them within moments.

Water dripped off Davy's nose, off his jaw, from his ears, from his fingers. It trickled down his spine, across his belly, from under his arms. It plastered his buckskin shirt to his torso, made his leggings cling to his legs. He could not have been more wet if he had jumped into a lake.

Since it was pointless to go back, Davy forged on. Not having the sun or landmarks to guide him, he relied on his inner compass to hold to a southerly bearing. Like most frontiersmen worthy of the name, he had an above-average sense of direction. Blindfold him, then spin him around, and nine times out of ten he could still tell you which way was north, south, east, or west. Exactly how he did it was a mystery. He just figured it stemmed from having spent so much time in the wilds, where a man had to learn to find his way around, or die.

His grandmother had been of the opinion that some people were like birds. That they had something inside of them which was the equivalent of a compass needle. Drop them anywhere, anytime, and they could find their way home, just like homing pigeons.

Whatever the case, Davy bent his steps southward. The crunch of hail underfoot was like the crunch of a bone in a coon dog's powerful jaws. Soon the hail grew slippery from the rain, and so much steam began to rise, it was akin to being in a sweat hole.

Flavius was as glum as a chickadee at a cat convention. He felt slimy, as if he were a salamander that had just wriggled up out of mud. Slogging through the hail, he muttered to himself, cursing his stupidity, his fickle nature, and the general state of human existence. It was unfair, he reflected, for the Almighty to beset His children with so many hardships. What had he ever done to deserve all this? He wasn't a sinner. Well, not much of one, anyhow. And Matilda made damn sure that he attended church as regular as clockwork.

That ought to count for something, Flavius thought. A year or so of no aggravation would be nice. A year of peace and tranquillity, where Matilda didn't nag him, where the cabin did not need any fixing up, and his in-laws did not pay a visit. A year where the crops grew themselves, the cows milked themselves, and ale at the tavern was always on the house.

"What happens if we can't find our horses?" Becky asked.

"We will," Davy said. Sometimes the girl was too inquisitive for her own good. It was better if she had no inkling of the nightmare they were in store for.

The rain tapered to a drizzle. To the southwest a rent split the clouds and a dazzling sunbeam penetrated, sparkling like a column of fireflies. A golden glow suffused the clouds around it, lending the scene an angelic aspect.

Becky cooed like a dove. "Isn't that pretty?"

Davy was more interested in locating the horses. The rain had melted much of the hail, but the ground was empty of tracks. Not so much as a scuff mark to give him a clue. Cradling Liz in the crook of his left elbow, he roved in a loop to the southwest. "Keep your eyes skinned," he said. "There should be some sign."

"My toes are all squishy," Becky commented.

"If you feel a chill, you let me know," Heather advised.

The last thing they needed was for the child to catch her death. Davy wished he could get a fire going to warm her, but there was nothing on hand to burn. The grass would not dry out for hours.

Which reminded Davy of the time. It was late afternoon. In three or four hours the sun would set. They had no food, no water, no kindling. Unless they stumbled on another wash or gully, they would spend the night exposed to the blustery wind. By morning they would be chilled to the marrow and hungry enough to eat worms. Having gone without before, he could get by. Flavius, too, although he would grumble to high heaven. But what about Heather and Becky? How well would they hold up?

"Look there!"

Becky was pointing to the west where a four-legged form was silhouetted against the sky. Davy squinted but could not determine whether it was a horse, a buffalo, a bear, or God-knew-what. "We'll take a look-see," he announced.

David L. Robbins

The girl smiled, then sniffled. Gamely, she limped along at her mother's side, the two hand in hand.

The sight made Flavius more upset. In his opinion, suffering should be doled out to those who earned it. Scoundrels, for instance, bandits and murderers and their ilk, they were the ones who should be afflicted, not decent folk, not innocents like Rebecca Dugan. She had never harmed a soul, yet she was fated to go through life a cripple. Was that fair? Was that right? What sort of God allowed such an injustice?

Giving a start, Flavius looked around. He had better be careful. Matilda had warned him time and again that puny mortals had no business questioning the Almighty. It wasn't fitting. Their paltry minds were not able to comprehend the grand mysteries of Creation. To try to do so, to be so brazen, was an affront to their Maker.

Flavius shook his head to scatter his thoughts. Deep thinking was a habit he had shunned, for his own health. Sometimes it gave him an awful headache. Just as arithmetic did back in school. All that adding and subtracting and dividing had made his head spin.

The ABCs were no better. One day he had startled Miss Tuttle by raising his hand and asking a question. A question that seemed logical to him. "Why are there twenty-six letters in the alphabet, ma'am? Why not twenty-five? Or twenty-seven? Or fifty? Or seventy-eight?"

"Each letter corresponds to a sound," Miss Tuttle had answered.

"But we can make more sounds than there are letters." To prove his point, Flavius had swelled out his chest and croaked like a bullfrog, not once but several times, then said proudly, "See? How come we don't have a letter for that?"

Half the class nearly busted a gut laughing. The other half rolled on the floor or were doubled over their desks. As for Miss Tuttle, she brayed until she had tears coming out of her eyes. It was the last question Flavius ever asked in class.

"It's a horse," Heather declared.

That it was. Davy recognized the sorrel, grazing by its lonesome. The dun and the bay, evidently, had gone their separate ways, which compounded the task of retrieving them. Anxious to do so before nightfall, Davy broke into a run. "I'll fetch him," he said. But it was not to be. For as soon as he was within earshot, the sorrel raised its head, pricked its ears, snorted, and pranced off at a brisk walk.

Davy ran faster. So did the sorrel. He called out, but the horse ignored him. When he slowed, so did the contrary critter. When he halted, it resumed its interrupted meal. Taking deep breaths, Davy slowly advanced. "It's all right, big fella," he said soothingly. "I don't aim to hurt you. Be a good boy and don't run off."

The horse let him approach within half a dozen steps, then nickered and cantered westward a stone's throw. Davy should have known. The whole day had been one jinx after another. He would be lucky if he caught the animal by midnight. Calming himself, he moved slowly forward. The sorrel was standing sideways so it could keep an eye on him without having to lift its head, and sure enough, when he was the same distance away as before, it whinnied and trotted to the southwest.

"Mangy flea-ridden nag."

The pattern was repeated so often, Davy was heartily tempted to put a ball into the animal. His patience stretched to the breaking point, he marked the sinking of the sun and the gathering of twilight. Once more he carefully neared his quarry, which had its hindquarters toward him for the first time. He was five feet off when the animal snorted and took a step.

Davy lunged, grabbing the tail. The sorrel looked back and hiked a rear leg to kick. In two bounds Davy was at the saddle. Grasping the horn, he swung up. The instant he did, the sorrel meekly hung its head, acting like a boy who had been caught with a hand in the cookie jar. Wary of a trick, Davy flicked the reins and turned the horse around. It did exactly as he wanted—no bucking, no biting, no fuss.

Gazing northward, Davy was appalled to see the plain empty. Intent on catching the horse, he had unwittingly left Flavius and the others far behind. That was soon remedied. Slamming his heels against the sorrel much harder than was called for, he hurried back. At any moment he expected to spot his companions.

A mile later, Davy wasn't so confident. He had seen neither hide nor hair of them, and it was now so dark that he could not track them without the aid of a torch. Cupping a hand to his mouth, he bawled Flavius's name again and again. There was no answer. Baffled, he drew rein and probed the darkness.

"*Now* what?"

Half a mile to the west, Flavius Harris hunkered beside the pitiful pile of partially dry brush he had collected. "Don't fret," he assured Heather and Becky Dugan. "I'll have us warm in two shakes of a lamb's tail."

Taking a tinderbox from his possibles bag, Flavius opened it and placed some punk close to the brush. He was partial to bits of dried maple, which he had accumulated on their canoe trip down the mighty Mississippi. Striking his fire steel against a big piece of flint he had brought from Tennessee, he produced sparks. Soon he had puffs of smoke rising from the tinder. Fanning it lightly with his breath, he kindled the brush into flame, then sat back to admire his handiwork.

They were in a gully that ran from north to south. The east slope was as high as Flavius was tall, the west side half that high. He had not wanted to stop, but Becky had been shivering and chattering like a squirrel having a fit. While Heather did her best to keep the girl from growing worse, Flavius had scrounged for what little dry vegetation there was to be had. He was always on the lookout for Davy, but his friend never showed up.

Flavius was confident it was only a matter of time. Davy

could track a turtle across solid rock. Finding the proverbial needle in a haystack was child's play for him. All they had to do was sit tight. Presently Crockett would come riding out of the night, and probably scold them for falling so far behind.

It was not as if Flavius had planned it. He had been chatting with Heather, hearing her tell about St. Louis, prying her for details of the wild shenanigans for which the city was famous. It had no law, to speak of. But it did boast more taverns, saloons, and sundry dives than any city east of the Mississippi, except maybe New Orleans.

Heather had been going on about an attempt by the genteel element to bring some order and culture to the city when Flavius happened to glance up and discover that Davy and the stupid horse were gone. He was afraid he had strayed far afield, but by then it was too dark to search for prints, and shortly afterward Becky had taken to shaking something terrible. So when they came across the gully, Flavius ushered them into it. Now here they were, crouched close to a fire that was giving off more smoke than heat. "Any second now it should catch," he said.

"I'm so cold," Becky said.

"There, there, dear." Heather held her child to her bosom, stroking Becky's hair. "You'll be fine." Her palm strayed across the girl's forehead, and Heather stiffened. She looked at Flavius in alarm.

The Tennessean understood. Becky had a fever, a high fever. And there was not a damn thing they could do. Matilda was knowledgeable about herbs and such, but both she and her herbs were a thousand miles away. Flavius had not brought any with him, since he so seldom felt poorly.

Hot broth would help. Unfortunately, all their cooking utensils were on the horses. Flavius stood and paced, racking his brain. He had no coat to share, no blankets to cover her with.

"Flavius. The fire."

It was sputtering and hissing, on the verge of going out. Quickly Flavius knelt and blew on the strands and branches still ablaze. The flames had to be coaxed to full life, gently, almost tenderly, as a man coaxed a shy animal from out of its den. By slow degrees the fire grew, the welcome warmth spread.

Becky leaned so near to the fire that Flavius feared she would burst into flame herself.

Heather was in the grip of stark anxiety. With an arm over her child's shoulders, she gulped and locked eyes that bespoke mute appeal on Flavius.

"I'll check down this gully for more stuff to burn."

He had gone fifty or sixty feet when it occurred to him that he should have left his rifle or a pistol. Then again, he was not venturing far. They would be fine. Roving along the murky, winding gulch, he groped every clump of weeds and each cluster of grass to see if they were dry enough to use. Most were not. He despaired of finding enough to last the night. Then, as he straightened from examining a grassy thatch that had sprouted in a niche, he spotted what appeared to be a row of trees to the west.

Clambering out, Flavius crawled low. He would move an elbow, pause to look and listen, then move a leg, then pause again. The shapes loomed higher, confirming that they were indeed trees. Here was all the firewood they'd need.

A slender young cottonwood was on the outer fringe. Once behind it, Flavius rose. There had been a time when he would have blindly bumbled on, setting himself up as a perfect target. But traveling with Davy had taught him a thing or two. Creeping from trunk to trunk, he verified that no hostiles were present.

He also made a crucial discovery. Another uneven line of cottonwoods grew twenty feet or so west of those he was in. Weaving toward them, he felt his left foot sink into clinging mud. Flavius jerked free, only to step in water when he shifted. What he had mistaken for a meandering ribbon of shadow was in truth the poorest excuse for a creek he had ever come across.

Only a couple of feet in width and a few inches deep, it was likely one of those that flowed only part of the year. Davy had told him about these infrequent waterways, how they were fed by runoff from the Rocky Mountains countless leagues to the west.

Flavius tried to imagine mountains so high they were crowned by snow twelve months of the year, mountains two to three *miles* in height, peaks so tall that no one had ever scaled them. He couldn't. The mountains of Tennessee were the highest he'd ever seen, and most of those were more like hills that had grown too big for their britches. They were rounded at the top and covered with forest, not like the jagged, barren peaks Davy claimed were common in the Rockies.

There was one place, at the eastern edge of Tennessee, that had the distinction of being the highest in the state. More than a mile high, folks said. But now that he thought about it, that mountain was rounded off like all the others.

Dipping a hand in the creek, Flavius tested the water. It was rather warm and had an earthy taste, but it would do. How to get some to the girl? He could fill his hat, but he couldn't carry his hat and his rifle at the same time. And he wasn't about to leave the gun there.

He compromised. Ranging among the trees, he picked up enough wood to build a sizable fire, wedging it between his forearms and his chest. The rifle went in his right hand. Thus burdened, Flavius hurried eastward. He planned to get the child nice and warm, leave his rifle with Heather, and come back for the water.

It had been about twenty yards from the cottonwoods to the gully. Flavius paced off the distance—but no gully. Puzzled, he went another ten paces. Still no gully. Suspecting he had drifted to the south, he hiked fifteen yards to the north. No gully. Completely confounded, he rotated to get a

45

fix on his position by the trees. Only, he couldn't see them.

"What the hell?" Flavius said aloud. Had he gotten turned around somehow? A scan of the heavens was of no benefit. Enough clouds were left to hide the Big Dipper, the one constellation he could identify. "This can't be happening."

Fighting a tide of panic, Flavius put himself in Davy's boots. What would the Irishman do in the same predicament? The answer: walk in ever-widening circles until he found the trees or the gully. Tickled with himself, Flavius started to do so, but first he set a log down to mark where he had started. His delight was boundless when he completed the first and ended up next to the log.

"Once again," Flavius said, only this time he walked in a much larger loop. In due course he completed it, or believed that he had, but the log was nowhere around. "It has to be here," he muttered at the night. The dark made a liar of him. He searched and searched and could not find it.

"Damn, damn, damn." Annoyed, Flavius moved at random. Far to the right, far to the left, at sharp angles one from the other. He must have gone twice the distance necessary, yet no cottonwoods, no stream, no gully.

The notion of being lost and alone set his heart to fluttering. Flavius was not a coward, not by any standard. He had fought bravely in one of the fiercest battles of the Creek War. He had stood by Davy's side again and again against overwhelming odds. But, like a stallion, he was easily spooked by certain things. Snakes, for one. He despised them, the mere sight being enough to make his skin crawl. Heights were another. Once he had climbed to the top of an enormous tree and nearly fainted when he looked down.

Becoming lost was another experience Flavius could well do without. He spun this way and that, then commenced running. To one side, to another. Back and forth. In circles. Panting, sweating, he dashed around like a madman. He flung the firewood down, then tripped over one of the logs a minute later when he ran past the same spot.

So unnerved was he that when he ran past a tree, it was several seconds before the fact sank in. Digging in his heels, he spun and sprinted back. He had blundered on a cottonwood. Grasping it as a drowning man might grasp a bobbing object that would keep him afloat, Flavius willed his nerves to steady. The creek must be close by, and he was thirsty enough to drink it dry.

Always keeping an eye on the cottonwood, Flavius took five steps in one direction, then five in another, and five in yet another. Inexplicably, the creek was not where it should be. At a loss to explain it, he looked for the rest of the trees and was shocked to learn that the one he had found was the only tree in his vicinity. The rest were nowhere around.

"I'm going insane," Flavius said softly. Now he had not only lost track of where the gully was, he had no notion of where the two rows of cottonwoods and the creek were. He had lost Davy, lost Heather, and lost Becky. The final insult to his dignity was that he had lost the firewood as well.

"My pride be damned," Flavius declared, upset that he was talking to himself but more upset at having no one else to talk to. Throwing his head back, he bawled, *"Mrs. Dugan! Can you hear me? Can anyone hear me?"*

A coyote did. It yipped long and loud. Flavius hefted his rifle, hoping the varmint would draw closer. As famished as he was, even coyote meat sounded appetizing. Then he was jolted by a disturbing suspicion. What if it hadn't been a coyote? What if it had been a hostile warrior, signaling others?

Darting to the tree, Flavius crouched with his back to the slender bole and cocked his long gun. They would not lift what little hair he had left without a struggle. As Davy was so fond of saying, it was root hog or die.

"Davy," Flavius whispered. Where in tarnation had Crockett gotten to? Had the hostiles already disposed of him?

The coyote yipped again.

Chapter Four

Davy Crockett had been through runs of bad luck before, but none of them, not a single, solitary one, rivaled this latest string. He had recovered the sorrel but could not find Flavius and the others. For hours he crisscrossed the prairie, without result. His fertile imagination leaped to several conclusions: they had become lost and wandered astray; they had been attacked by a grizzly or a pack of ravenous wolves; hostile Indians had taken them prisoner; or, the one he favored, the one he prayed was the case, they had holed up somewhere, in another wash maybe, in which case he would not find them until daylight.

So, reluctantly, along about midnight, Davy reined up on the lee side of a high knoll. Stripping off the saddle, he securely hobbled the sorrel, and as an added precaution he tied a rope around its neck and the other end around his leg. He would not risk losing the animal a second time. Exhaustion dulled his worry. Curled up in a blanket, he was soon asleep.

Davy slept fitfully. He dreamed of harrowing clashes with animals and men. One involved a band of Indians who ate human flesh. They had captured him and were dragging him toward a huge black pot filled with boiling water, when he woke up in a cold sweat.

Dawn was about to break. To the east a pale glow rimmed the horizon. Rising stiffly, he stretched and did knee bends to limber up. Then, after throwing on the saddle, he mounted and rode northward in search of tracks.

Dew moistened the virgin grassland. He was so thirsty that after a while he stopped, tore a strip from the blanket, and used it as a sponge to soak up water and wring it into a cup. When the cup was full, he drank slowly, relishing every mouthful. People tended to take basics like food and water for granted. It was only when they were deprived of those basics that they fully appreciated how precious nourishment was.

Going on, Davy roamed far and wide. He came across the prints of antelope, of deer, of elk, of wolves and coyotes and a painter, of a black bear, of a mother grizzly and her cub, of rabbits and quail and prairie dogs, of sparrows and robins and crows, of a hawk and a small owl, but nowhere did he find those he was searching for.

It was downright aggravating. Davy halted again, pondering. Things were in a pretty considerable snarl, and he had no ready solution. The sun was two hours into the sky. What if he went the whole day and did not locate the others?

Refusing to abide glum thoughts, Davy rode westward. He had gone a mile or so when a stick figure took solid form in the distance. A tree—a lone tree, he assumed at first—and he made for it. Where there were trees, there was water. And game. Images of food on the hoof made his mouth water. He had not eaten in so long that his stomach growled constantly, like an irate wolverine.

He was a couple of hundred yards out when something struck him as strange. The base of the tree was broader than it should be, given the slim trunk. A brownish tint hinted that an animal of some sort was resting there. A deer maybe, Davy speculated, and tucked Liz to his shoulder.

At a range of one hundred yards, the animal stirred. Davy saw it shift, saw a limb move. It was on the other side of the tree, so he could not quite make out what it was yet. But he was ninety percent convinced it was indeed a whitetail.

At fifty yards misfortune struck again. The horse snorted.

Flavius Harris was lost in dreamland. He was home, in his cabin, seated at the table. Matilda had whipped up a feast to celebrate his homecoming, and spread out before him was heaven on earth, enough food for a regiment. Roast venison, roast turkey, fried chicken. Beans and turnips and beets. Taters covered by thick gravy. Corn on the cob smothered in butter. Bread so fresh, its aroma was intoxicating. Two pies, cherry and apple, and a cake. He could not make up his mind which to eat first. Finally choosing the turkey, he helped himself to a leg and raised it to his mouth. He was delirious with ecstasy.

A noise awakened him. Flavius could not say what it had been, but he knew it had come from close by. He lay still, listening, and heard the clomp of hooves. *Indians,* he figured, and sat bolt upright. The sound came from behind him, from behind the tree. Whirling, he snapped up his gun, cocked the hammer, and fired, all in the blink of an eye.

Too late, Flavius saw who it was. His rifle boomed and bucked, and in horror he watched as Davy Crockett toppled from the sorrel onto the hard earth. "Nooooo!" Flavius wailed, leaping to his feet. He dashed madly to the spot, raw terror eating at his innards. He had killed the best friend he ever had! He had murdered a man who was more like a brother to him than his own brothers! Worst of all, he had rubbed out the one person who could see him safely back to Tennessee.

Flavius sank onto a knee and gripped the Irishman's shoul-

51

der. "I'm sorry! I'm so sorry!" he said, rolling Davy over.

"You should be, you danged nuisance."

The hand that slapped Flavius across the cheek was a blur. Rocked onto his heels, he broke out in a broad grin. "You're alive! Praise the Lord, you're alive!"

"No thanks to you." Davy sat up and brushed grass from his hunting shirt. At the last moment he had seen who it was and held his own fire. He'd had a split-second warning before Flavius shot, enough for him to dive off the sorrel and save himself. Even so, the ball had whizzed dangerously near to his chest as he fell. "How many times must I tell you to always be sure of your target before you squeeze the trigger?"

"I know, I know," Flavius said. He was so happy at being reunited that he didn't care if Davy bent his ear. He deserved it.

"Remember what happened to Meriwether Lewis?" Davy mentioned. Everyone had heard about the famous Lewis and Clark expedition, and how one of their own men had accidentally shot Lewis, mistaking him for an elk. "And my uncle?"

Flavius had heard the story a dozen times. The uncle had gone deer hunting and saw what he took for a deer in a patch of grapes. Only it was a neighbor, whom the uncle shot through the body. "I know, I know," he repeated impatiently, then on an impulse he threw his arms around Crockett and gave him a mighty hug. "Wallop me with a rock if you want. Skin me alive. This coon is floating on clouds."

Davy shrugged free and stood. "You're worse than my kids sometimes, you know that?" Picking up Liz, he inspected her to make sure she was not damaged. On straightening, he was surprised to see that Heather and Becky had not come running at the shot. "Where are . . . ?" he began.

"I lost them," Flavius bleated, staying where he was. He'd be harder to hit on the ground.

"You what?"

Flavius could not help himself. The words spilled from him like milk from an overturned pitcher. "Late last night. We made camp in a gully, and I went for some fuel for the fire. By a sheer fluke I came across some trees and a creek. So I loaded up on wood and headed back, but for the life of me I couldn't find them. Hell, I couldn't even find the gully. I tried and tried, for hours. Honest to God, I did." He was so upset, his voice quavered.

Davy rested a hand on his friend's shoulder. "It's all right. I know you tried your best. Now let's see if we can backtrack."

Standing, Flavius said, "The first thing we need to do is find two rows of cottonwoods. That's where the creek was."

"There are some cottonwoods over that way," Davy said, and pointed at a barely visible long line of trees and brush an arrow's flight to the west.

Flavius was flabbergasted. "That's where they been the whole damn time?" he blurted. Dazed, he moved toward the vegetation. "I must have gone past them a hundred times and not realized it. Damn me for being the biggest fool ever born!"

Davy did not waste another moment. Mounting, he caught up with Flavius and extended an arm. "Climb up. They're probably worried half sick about us."

The mention jarred Flavius's memory. Awkwardly clambering on, he held on to the cantle and said, "That reminds me. The little girl is ill."

"What?"

"She was shaking like a leaf and had a bad fever," Flavius explained. "That's why I left them in the first place. I wanted to make her nice and warm with a big fire."

Being sick in the wilderness was a grave matter. There were no doctors, no hospitals, no medicines. A person did not have the luxury of lying abed for days or weeks until healed. Becoming seriously ill was often a death sentence, as surely as if someone plunged cold steel into the heart.

Friendly Indians sometimes helped out, as had happened to Davy once, well before he left on this gallivant. While hunting with friends, he had been stricken by a bout of a mysterious malady. His companions had left him for dead, a callous betrayal of trust he never forgave—especially when he later learned that one of them had secretly hankered after his wife, and that was why they had deserted him.

He would have gone to meet his Maker. No doubt in his mind. But some Indians he did not even know came along and kindly carried him to the home of a Quaker woman, who nursed him back to health. He would always remember those Indians. It was why he did not share the common view that all red men were vermin and should be exterminated.

But now no friendly Indians were handy. Little Becky must get plenty of rest and food to keep her strength up, or they would be digging a small grave before too long. Davy trotted to the cottonwoods. They followed the stream north a couple of hundred feet to a mud bar bearing jumbled footprints.

"That's where I sank in," Flavius said.

Davy hurried, bending down low to the ground to better read the sign. The tracks came from the east, and it was not long before he located the gully. Riding down into it, he galloped northward.

Flavius was happy that everything had worked out just dandy. They would have Becky fit as a fiddle in no time, and soon they would be on their way to the Mississippi. Then St. Louis, and home. Wouldn't it be grand, he thought, if Matilda had a feast waiting for him, just like in his dream? All that food! The juicy turkey, the roast corn on the cob, those delicious pies, and that—

"Is this the spot?"

They were there so soon? Flavius looked down. Charred strands of grass were all that remained of the small fire. A few prints and scuff marks indicated where the mother and daughter had huddled beside it. "Yep," he answered, elated.

Then he realized that the two were nowhere to be seen. "But what happened to Heather and Becky?"

"That's what I'd like to know." Swinging a leg over the saddle, Davy slid off. To a seasoned tracker, reading footprints was as simple as reading a book. Heather and Rebecca had sat side by side for a couple of hours. Every now and then Heather had risen. Her tracks led to random clumps of grass she had fed to the flames. Davy guessed that she had kept the fire going for a couple of hours after Flavius left. At last it went out, and Heather had risen and paced in a circle. She had been worried about Flavius, Davy deduced, but more worried about Becky. The girl had been lying still, curled into a ball. Her mother curled up around her to add warmth. They must have spent a harrowing night, Heather fearing the worst.

At daybreak they had risen. One set of tracks led to the west. Their size and depth revealed that Heather had been carrying Becky. Apparently the child was too weak to get about on her own.

Remounting, Davy trailed them. He was at a loss to understand why Heather had picked that particular direction. She knew Flavius had gone south. The length of her strides showed that she had been moving swiftly, practically running at times. Where did she think she was going?

Over a low rise, in a wide gulch rimmed by dry brush, lay the answer. From the rim the Tennesseans saw evidence of another fire, and hoofprints.

"Someone was here," Flavius said, stating the obvious.

"Heather must have seen the smoke and mistook it for one of us," Davy deduced. Kneeing the sorrel down the slope, he felt the nape of his neck prickle. The hoofprints were those of unshod horses. "Indians."

"Oh, Lord." Flavius swiveled to survey the plain. "A war party, you reckon?" He recalled the many tales of atrocities blamed on Indians, of white women taken captive and never seen again, of captives ruthlessly butchered, or worse. Most of the tales were tavern gossip, the kind of stories men swapped when they had imbibed a bit too much. But they filled him with cold dread.

It took Davy a while to put the pieces together. Eight warriors had ridden in from the southwest the evening before. They had been in no particular hurry, riding in single file—a practice of men on the warpath. The warriors made camp and spent the night quietly. Normally they would have left at the crack of dawn, but Davy noticed that one of the horses had been limping when it arrived, and he had a hunch the Indians had put off leaving to tend to the stricken animal.

It must have shocked them immensely when Heather blundered onto their camp. A white woman and child, where no whites had any business being. She had tried to flee, but several had overtaken her and dragged her back. One had carried Becky.

"They left less than an hour ago," Davy concluded.

"Then we have a chance to catch them," Flavius said.

That they did, even riding double. The frontiersmen trotted to the southwest under the bright sun, their hunger forgotten, their thirst ignored. The need to save their friends eclipsed all else. Davy verified that his pistols were loaded and primed, then loosened the tomahawk under his belt. As much as he would like to have Heather and Becky returned without bloodshed, it was unlikely the warriors would be so inclined.

The Irishman was not able to judge exactly how long it would take to catch up. Two factors were in their favor, though, one being that an Indian mount was going lame, the other that Heather and Becky would have to ride double with separate warriors, further slowing the war party down.

Worry for the girl gnawed at Davy. She was a sweet, spunky, wonderful child who had gone through more than her share of hardships but had not let them break her spirit. Should something happen to her—He erased the idea from his mind, refusing to harbor it. Becky would be fine. She had to be.

Each minute was weighed down by an anchor. Davy chafed at their slow progress, while in reality he pushed the sorrel a bit too recklessly.

The Indians never deviated from their southwesterly heading. Who they were, where they hailed from, was a mystery.

In Tennessee, Davy had been able to tell one tribe from another by the differences in their moccasins. No two tribes fashioned their footwear exactly alike. Some had wide soles, some had narrow. Some had curved soles, some were straight. It was the same west of the Mississippi, but he was not versed in the style of the respective tribes here.

For all he knew, he was wrong. The war party might really be a party of harmless hunters who were taking Heather and Becky to their village so the child could be treated for her illness.

And cows could fly.

By midday it was apparent that they would not see hide nor hair of the Indians before nightfall, if then. They had been an hour behind at the outset; they were still an hour behind. The sorrel was flagging, so Davy had Flavius climb off and the two of them walked for half an hour to give the horse a breather.

Flavius was sore and tired and hungry enough to eat grass, but he did not complain. He was fond of Heather, even more fond of Becky. She had always treated him decently, and any sacrifice that must be made to save her was fine by him. "If either is harmed, there'll be hell to pay," he remarked.

Davy shared the sentiment, but he was willing to acknowledge that the Indians might not be to blame, not if Rebecca was as sick as Flavius had let on. There was only so much the warriors could do, if they were disposed to do anything. Becky meant nothing to them. They might abandon her to die, afraid that whatever afflicted her was contagious, and Davy could not blame them. It was common knowledge that whites carried diseases against which the red race had no immunity. Smallpox was one example; it had wiped out more Indians than all the guns ever made.

"There's a good side to this," Flavius commented. "Play our cards right, and each of us can end up with a horse of our own."

"Play them wrong, and the buzzards will feast tomorrow."

"We've got it to do, regardless."

Davy had no argument there. He would not rest until the females were safe, even if that entailed following the war party clear to Mexico. How well he remembered the ordeal his uncle James had gone through. Captured by the Creeks, James spent over seventeen years among the tribe. He gained his freedom when, by sheer coincidence, Davy's father learned that James was alive and bought him from an Indian trader.

It had taken James many months to adjust to being among his own kind. Some whispered that he never did. Whatever the case, James devoted the rest of his life to searching for the secret silver mine of the Creeks—a mine neither he nor anyone else ever found.

Davy knew of other whites taken captive. Usually, men were killed outright. The lucky ones were adopted. As for the women, whether adopted or not, invariably they endured a fate worse than death, a stigma so vile that they refused to be rescued or purchased if the chance arose. This was particularly true of those who gave birth while in captivity. They would rather stay with their captors than endure the shame heaped on their shoulders should they return to "civilized" society.

Davy would spare Heather that outrage. Becky was too young for breeding. Among most tribes on both sides of the Mississippi, girls were not married off until they had their first monthly—or their first "visit from Flo," as the ladies in his neck of the woods were fond of saying.

It was one of the longest afternoons of Davy's life. In a

way he was glad they did not spot the war party before nightfall. The Indians might well have spotted Flavius and him first, nipping their rescue in the bud. As it turned out, the sun had relinquished the sky to the stars when a tiny pinpoint of earthbound light prompted Davy to rein up. "Yonder they are," he announced.

Flavius had been dozing. He couldn't help himself. Fatigue seeped from every pore in his body, and his eyelids were as heavy as lead. On hearing Davy, he roused himself with an effort and focused on the campfire. "Should we go in with our guns blazing?"

It was not as silly as it sounded. They would drop two or three with their first volley. Maybe convince the rest that a superior force was attacking. Spook them into running off. Then again, the warriors might rally, and Davy had no desire to end his days so far from Tennessee, his carcass left to rot. "We'll wait until they bed down."

What to do with the sorrel? Davy mused. They might need to make a hasty retreat, so it was prudent to leave the horse untied. But the ornery critter might wander off while they were gone. Against his better judgment, he hobbled it.

Flavius was as nervous as a buck being stalked by hunters, but he did not let on, not with precious lives at stake. Little was said during the next four hours. Presently the moment of truth arrived. Swallowing hard, he cat-footed after Davy. They were more than a mile from the camp. By the time they were close enough to note details, he was so winded that his attention lapsed and he bumped into his friend when Davy unexpectedly halted. It earned him a severe look.

The eight horses were in a string to the north of the fire. Six of the warriors were asleep. An elderly man and a short one were by the fire, talking in low tones. South of the fire were Heather and Becky, the mother in misery, seated with her daughter's head in her lap.

Davy studied the members of the war party. They were unlike any Indians he had ever seen. Swarthy, muscular,

59

well-proportioned, they wore leggings and moccasins but no shirts. Their shoulders and chests were painted with lines and symbols, as were their faces and foreheads. Most of their hair had been shaved, except for a strip high in the middle that had been slicked to stand straight up. It reminded Davy of porcupine quills. Eagle feathers were worn by several. Added decoration consisted of bead necklaces and bracelets. The leggings were fringed.

Flat on his belly, Davy waited for the last pair to turn in. The old one was relating something or other in a language that was so much Greek to Davy. Every warrior, he noted, was armed with a knife. Bows, quivers, and lances were scattered among the sleepers.

Suddenly Heather unfurled. Gesturing at the older warrior, she said, ''Please. My daughter is very ill. Something must be done or she'll die.''

The men stopped talking, the oldest regarding her intently.

''I know you're the leader here,'' Heather told him. ''Help her, I beg you. She's burning up.'' To demonstrate, she placed her hand on Becky's brow, then pointed at the flickering flames.

The older warrior rose. Walking over, he pressed a callused palm to the girl's head. His features were a blank slate. Grunting, he walked back to the fire and sat.

''Damn you, you heathen!'' Heather railed. ''I'm not going to sit here and let her die! Either do something, or so help me, you'll regret it!''

Her outburst woke up every last warrior. Some glanced at the captives, muttered, and went back to sleep. Several sat up. A long talk ensued, the older warrior doing most of it. Repeated looks were cast at mother and daughter, looks that did not bode well. At length the men lay back down. Davy was glad when the leader turned in too. But the short warrior stayed up, a bow next to him, a quiver across his back.

Flavius had not reckoned on a sentry being posted. It complicated things. His heart went out to Heather, who was slumped over Becky, her shoulders quaking as she silently sobbed. He looked at Davy, but his friend did not motion for them to move in. Soon, Flavius hoped. Before he was too tired to be of any use.

The short warrior drew his knife and honed it on a whetstone just like the one in Davy's possibles bag. He wondered if the warrior had taken it from a dead white, or traded for it. The man stroked the edge of the blade smoothly, engrossed in the chore.

Davy folded his arms and rested his chin on his wrist. It would be another hour before they could do anything. The rest must be deep in slumber, the sentry's senses dulled by lack of activity.

Closing his eyes, Davy recalled his grandfather and grandmother, both dear people, both slaughtered in their home by rampaging Creeks. For years afterward he had hated Indians as feverishly as any white man alive did. Then came that day his illness laid him low and those Indians took him to the Quaker.

It was rare when a man knew he had gone through a major change in his life. Most changes took place gradually, building up over months or years, subtly altering character until the man was not the same as he had once been, without realizing a change had taken place. That day, though, was a major turning point in his life. It was the reason he would not shoot an Indian unless set upon. The reason he did not open fire on this bunch from ambush.

They had not harmed Heather or Becky, which was encouraging. Their painted faces and bodies, though, were proof they were a war party. Whether they were after scalps or out to count coup, as was the Sioux custom, was irrelevant. They would not take kindly to having their captives rescued. To avoid a bloodbath, he must resort to guile, to the wiles of a fox.

His left leg was nudged. Glancing around, Davy saw Flavius nod at the camp. The short warrior had risen and was stretching. As Davy looked on, the man circled the fire, then paused, facing them. They were safe enough, since they were too far away for the glow to illuminate them.

Why, then, did the warrior lean forward as if he had spotted something?

Why did he grip the hilt of his knife?

The man came toward them.

Chapter Five

Davy Crockett tensed, then slid his hand down his side to the tomahawk. He had to dispatch the warrior quietly and pray none of the others were light sleepers. Grasping the handle, he prepared to rise onto his knees. Countless hours spent in practice made him confident he could throw the weapon with extreme accuracy and bury it in the man's chest.

Flavius was ready to bolt at the first outcry. Outnumbered as they were, they would be swiftly overwhelmed. And since they could be of no help to Heather and Becky dead, he would rather flee so they could try again another day.

The warrior stopped, his eyebrows knit. Davy realized that the man was gazing *past* them. Whatever had drawn his interest was out on the prairie. Could it be the sorrel? Davy wondered. Although hobbled, the animal could move about a little. Had it drifted toward the camp, close enough to be observed? Davy could not turn to see, because the movement might give him away.

Clearly perplexed, the warrior took a few more steps. He slowly relaxed and removed his hand from his knife. Quirking his mouth upward, he turned around and took his seat by the fire. Whatever he had seen was either gone or had been a figment of his imagination.

Davy did not replace the tomahawk. He might need it before the night was done. Staying where he was, he bided his time, exercising the patience of a panther.

The sentry let the fire burn low but not out. Arms folded, the man tried his best to stay awake. Every so often his eyes would close, his chin would dip. Whenever it did, he jerked his chin up again and shook himself. This happened a dozen times or more. Then he dozed off again and did not awaken.

Davy waited another five minutes for safety's sake. Shifting toward Flavius, he whispered, "You get the horses. I'll see to Heather and Becky."

Flavius would rather it was the other way around. Horses had a nasty habit of nickering at the wrong moment. But Davy angled to the left and was gone, crawling silently, before Flavius could say anything.

Snaking to the right, Flavius gave a wide berth to the pale glow that bathed the grass. When the horses were between him and the sleepers, he rose into a crouch. Most of the animals were also asleep. A bay had its head up and was peering to the south. Possibly, it had heard Davy—which amused Flavius. Usually, he was the one who made too much noise. Slinking toward the west end of the string, he congratulated himself on outdoing his friend.

The bay tried to turn toward him. Flavius heard it sniff loudly a few times. He had forgotten about the wind, which was blowing his scent right to them. Afraid the bay would whinny, he froze. The bay gave its mane a toss, bobbed its head, and pawed the ground. Flavius did not like that one bit. The darned critter would agitate the whole blamed string. Sucking in a breath, he marshaled his courage and boldly rose. Advancing slowly so as not to scare it, he whispered,

"No need to be afraid, fella. I'm as peaceable as they come."

The bay was not so sure. Just as horses owned by whites grew accustomed to the scent of their owners and became agitated when they caught the scent of Indians, so these animals were accustomed to the odor of Indians and regarded that of whites as they would the odor of a roving cougar or a bear. The bay tried to back away. Brought up short by the rope, it pawed the earth again.

Flavius stopped to avoid upsetting it further. One of the sleepers moved, draping an arm across his chest. Another mumbled. Flavius glimpsed Davy across the way, close to Heather and her daughter.

The Irishman had seen what the bay was doing, and halted. It would not take much to bring the warriors to their feet, brandishing their weapons. The sentry was sleeping soundly enough, but was bent so far forward that he might pitch over.

When neither of the woodsmen made any threatening moves, the bay calmed. Flavius felt safe in edging near enough to gently touch its muzzle. The horse sniffed his fingers, then his sleeve. Rubbing it, he sidled to the rope. None of the other animals showed the least interest in him.

Davy sank onto his stomach and made like an eel. Reaching Heather, he plucked at her dress. She did not react. Cautiously rising onto a knee, he pushed her arm. She smacked her lips and moved the arm but did not wake up. Taking a gamble, he clamped a hand over her mouth and pulled her off Becky, urgently whispering in her ear, "Don't cry out! It's me, Davy!"

Heather had gone rigid and clawed at his hand, only to relent when he identified himself. She turned, whispered, "Thank God!" and pressed her face against his neck. He felt moisture dampen his skin. "I've been so afraid. I'm at my wit's end."

"Shhhhh," Davy said. He was surprised that she had not been bound. Maybe the warriors figured she was not about to desert her ailing child. Peeling Heather off, he gave her the rifle, then scooped Becky up.

Across the camp, Flavius had untied four of the horses and was working on the fifth. The bay was one of those he had freed. Without any warning, the horse abruptly wheeled and pranced into the night—almost brushing the sentry. The man leaped erect, blinked in confusion on seeing the animal loose, and took a step after it.

Davy was backpedaling into the darkness, but he was not quite quick enough.

The warrior whirled, a hand flying to the quiver on his back. A harsh shout ripped from his throat as he nocked a shaft to the sinew string.

Davy was helpless, his hands full, unwilling to drop Becky in order to draw a pistol. The other men were heaving upright, many talking all at once. The sentry sighted down the arrow, centering the barbed tip squarely on Davy.

Heather shot him. Liz boomed, belching lead and smoke, the impact smashing the bowman backward.

Simultaneously, several events occurred. The remaining warriors turned toward Davy, Becky, and Heather, fury and blood lust contorting their features. Flavius realized his friend's plight and did the only thing he could think of. He whooped and hollered and flapped his arms, sending the four horses into flight. They weaved among the warriors, creating confusion, causing several to leap aside, barreling one over.

Davy pivoted and fled. ''Run!'' he urged, racing flat out, listening for the buzz of feathered shafts and the swish of heavy lances. Heather kept pace, her dress swirling around her legs, her golden hair flying.

Flavius ran in the opposite direction. Thanks to the damn bay, everything had gone all to hell. A glance showed him that several of the warriors had gone after the horses, two were chasing Davy, and two were after *him*.

Terror lent wings to Flavius's feet. Pumping his arms and legs, he ran as he had never run before. Yet that would not be enough. His portly build rendered him less fleet than most men, and he had no illusions about the outcome.

The warriors were lean shapes in the gloom. Arrows rattled in their quivers. In the lead was a tall man who had the grace and speed of an antelope.

They're going to catch me! Flavius thought, and bit his lip to stifle an outcry. Losing his head would cost him his life. He had a rifle, didn't he? And a pair of loaded flintlocks? The savages would not take him without a struggle. He looked back to see if they had gained. The very next step, his right foot snagged on something and he was flung onto his face, thudding down so hard that his breath whooshed from his lungs.

It was a shallow rut, barely three feet wide and five feet long. Flavius placed his hands flat to push erect. Footsteps drummed, and he braced for the feel of iron fingers on his arms and neck. Instead, the tall warrior loped past a few yards to his left. Seconds later the other man hastened by on the right. They had not seen him fall!

Flavius watched as they dwindled in the darkness. When he could no longer see them, he rose and hurried to the southeast. One of the warriors was leading a pair of horses to the string, and the man who had been shot was being examined by another. Of Davy, Becky, and Heather there was no sign.

The sorrel was right where they had left it. Flavius removed the hobbles, stuffed them in the saddlebag, and climbed on. He would stay put until Davy showed. They had failed to obtain extra mounts, but they could get by. Provided they escaped.

To the northwest two warriors appeared, the tall one and the other. Somehow they had found him. Flavius lashed the reins and cut to the left as an arrow cleaved the space his head had just occupied. At a mad gallop he outdistanced them, speeding into the night until he was well out of bow range.

He aimed to go no more than a quarter of a mile, to stay relatively close to be of help to Davy. But when Flavius brought the sorrel to a stop and shifted in the saddle, the campfire had vanished. He rose in the stirrups and still could not see the flickering light. "I can't have gone that far," he declared. The only other explanation was that the Indians had extinguished it, which made sense if they believed they would be attacked again.

Where did that leave him? He had to find Davy, but he was averse to aimlessly roving the prairie. The last time he had gotten hopelessly lost, and might again. Or blunder onto some of the Indians.

Flavius dismounted. Wrapping the reins around his right wrist, he sat down. Once morning broke, he would hunt for his companions. Until then, he might as well make himself comfortable. *Where are you, Davy?* he thought. *Did they get you?*

The answer was no, but not from a lack of trying.

Three hundred yards southeast of the camp, Davy Crockett hunkered in a gulch. His lungs were raw, and pulsing blood hammered his temples. He had led the warriors on a merry chase, winding this way and that, flattening on occasion, rising when the coast seemed clear. Becky had not uttered a peep once. Nor had she awakened, which troubled him. At his side Heather was sprawled, a hand over her mouth to stifle her rasping gasps.

"Did we shake them?" she asked through clenched teeth.

"I don't rightly know," Davy confessed. Gently depositing Becky, he rose high enough to peek over the rim. The fire had gone out or been smothered. Quiet reigned, but he was not deceived. The war party would not give up easily. If he was in their moccasins, he'd regroup and commence a sweep at first light.

"How's Rebecca?"

Davy felt the girl's forehead. It was as hot as a red coal,

and when he lightly shook her, she did not respond. A bad sign. Wrapping the blanket tightly around her shoulders, he nestled the child in his lap and leaned back against the gulch wall. "She needs food and rest."

"Tell me something I don't know," Heather said testily. "She needs a hell of a lot more than that." Wringing her hands, she tilted her pale face to the sky. "What am I to do? Please don't let her die. She's my pride and joy."

"We'll do all we can."

"I wasn't talking to you. I was—"

A scuffling noise stilled her tongue. Davy carefully passed Becky to Heather, then slowly uncoiled, drawing a pistol. There had not been time to reload Liz. In the murk to the north something moved. A man, an animal, he could not say. It was soon gone. Earlier, he had heard a horse galloping to the southeast and took some small satisfaction in thinking that the warriors had lost at least one of their mounts.

Davy tucked the flintlock under his belt. He uncapped his powder horn, gripped Liz, and fed the proper amount of black powder into the barrel. Next he removed a ball from his ammo pouch. Wrapping a patch around the conical lead, he slid the ramrod from its housing, then tamped the ball down the barrel. As he finished, Heather started to softly weep. "Chin up," he whispered. "Where there's life, there's hope."

"Spare me the platitudes," she said bitterly. "I am sick and tired of always being told to look at the bright side. People like you don't seem to realize that sometimes there *is* no bright side."

"You sound as if you've lost faith."

"I never had much to begin with. Losing my father at an early age was a valuable lesson. It taught me that all the wishes in the world don't amount to an ounce of dog droppings." Heather bit her lower lip. "Then I met the man I married. He was so decent, so kind, so understanding. He treated me like a princess, he worked his fingers to the bone to provide for our family. His death nearly destroyed me. I would have slit my wrists if not for Becky.'' She choked off.

''No need to go on.''

''Isn't there?'' Heather snapped. ''Or don't you want to hear the brutal truth? Oh, sure, I met Jonathan Hamlin and fell in love all over again. But look at what happened to him! And now my darling daughter!'' She placed a hand on Becky. ''I swear to you, Davy Crockett, by all that's holy. If she doesn't pull through, I will refuse to live another day.''

''That's foolishness,'' Davy said. ''Life is too precious to be squandered.''

''Tell that to my husband. Tell that to Jonathan Hamlin.'' Heather's voice began to rise. ''Tell it to Becky!''

Davy thrust a hand over her mouth. ''Please,'' he said.

Heather swatted it aside. Livid, she clenched her fists and continued in a low growl. ''Life isn't a storybook, damn you. Our lives don't always have happy endings. Bad things happen to good people all the time. And it's not fair.''

''I know,'' Davy agreed, thinking of his grandparents and his first wife. ''We just have to take each day as it comes. Hardships make us stronger, if we let them.''

''More corny sayings,'' Heather spat. ''Words, words, words. What good do they do? Do they stop us from suffering? Will they spare Becky from being a cripple her whole life through? Words don't deliver us from evil. They numb us to it.''

Davy hesitated. It was hardly the right time or place to debate her outlook on life. Yet his intuition told him that she was close to the breaking point, that what she needed more than anything else was sincere encouragement. ''Look, I don't claim to have all the answers. I'm a backwoodsman, not a minister. You could count on two hands the number of times that I've set foot in a church.''

Heather glumly stroked Becky's hair.

''I lost my first wife, so I know what you've been through.

Losing a loved one has to be the worst experience ever. It tears us up inside, twists our innards until we want to scream. We think about giving up, about throwing ourselves off a cliff, or stepping in front of a speeding wagon.''

Her interest was piqued. ''Why didn't you?''

''I owed it to my children, and to myself. Life is precious. My ma used to teach us that we should always make the best of it. 'Don't squander your gift,' she'd say when we were sulking about one thing or another.'' Davy paused. ''It's like being thrown from a horse. Some folks never ride again. But those who want to make the most of what life has to offer get right back up and climb in the saddle.''

It was a while before Heather replied. Out of the blue, she commented, ''Both your wives were lucky women.''

''How's that?'' Davy thought they had been talking about Heather's relationships, not his own.

''Men like you are rare, Mr. Crockett. You have courage, wit, compassion, qualities every woman wants in her man but doesn't always find. My first husband was wonderful, but he lacked backbone. He wouldn't stand up to my step-father until it was too late. As for Jonathan, he loved me dearly, and I him, but as you saw for yourself, he wasn't the most competent person who ever lived.''

Davy did not see what any of this had to do with what they had discussed.

''Most women would never admit as much, but we draw strength from our men, just as men draw strength from us, I suspect. Think of us as plants that need water to thrive. We get that water, get our strength, from our loved ones. And when one of us loses the other, we wither, like a flower dying on a vine.'' She sighed. ''Does anything I've just said make sense?''

''I think I understand,'' Davy said.

Heather gazed at the myriad of stars. ''You're not the only one who doesn't have all the answers. I've always believed the Good Lord put us here for a purpose, but for the life of me, I have no idea what that purpose is. I thought I did, once. But the older I get, the more confused I become.''

Davy squeezed her hand, and she responded by quickly bending and kissing the back of his. ''What was that for?''

''For being here when I needed someone. For being a friend.'' Heather rested her head against the gulch wall and shut her eyes. ''I'm so tired. Please forgive me.''

''Get some rest,'' Davy told her. Rising, he scoured the plain for hostiles. And Flavius. In the confusion earlier, he had not seen where his friend got to. Since he had not heard any shots or screams, he reasoned that Flavius had eluded the warriors and was lying low somewhere. He regretted being separated again, but it could not be helped.

What he regretted even more was Heather being forced to kill that sentry. The war party would not leave the area until they avenged the loss. Come sunrise, the warriors would fan out, hunting.

But his immediate concern was Becky. Unless something was done, the girl might die. He seemed to recollect seeing a water skin in the Indian camp. It was a shame he had not thought to grab it at the outset.

Davy glanced at the mother and child. They slumbered soundly, the one so sick that she would not notice if a gun went off next to her ear, the other so exhausted that she slept the sleep of the dead. The starlight accented their pale skin, rendering them angelic in repose.

They needed a horse. Specifically, the sorrel. Without it, the likelihood of eluding the war party was mighty slim. Doubling over, Davy tenderly touched Becky's chin, then Heather's head. They should be safe enough while he was away, but he leaned Liz within easy reach of Heather, just in case.

Rotating, Davy stealthily scaled the gulch, crept into the grass, and bore to the east. The darkness did not dampen his homing instincts. He knew exactly where the sorrel was, and he estimated that it would take no more than twenty minutes to get there and back.

Wolves howled in the distance. A pack was on the prowl, but wolves rarely posed a threat to humans. When rabid, yes, and sometimes when they had not eaten for quite a while. Otherwise, they gave everything on two legs a wide berth.

Davy slowed when he heard rustling to his left. Leveling a pistol, he trained it on a patch of grass. The stems were waving from side to side, as they would if a warrior were crawling through them. A head appeared, with two of the longest ears on any creature this side of the Hereafter. A jackrabbit was foraging for succulent sweet shoots. It took a number of short hops, then nibbled a bit, its nose twitching. Davy did not budge. He took it for granted that the thing would catch wind of him and skedaddle, but it came steadily closer.

Davy thought of Becky. Switching the pistol to his left hand, he inched his right to the tomahawk. The jackrabbit did not notice. Blithely, it hopped nearer.

Like a predator about to pounce, Davy did not take his eyes off its short furry neck. A patch of grass at arm's length lured the unsuspecting creature over. He saw its stubby front paws, saw its large front teeth gnaw at the grass. And in a blur of motion, Davy arced the tomahawk up and around. The keen edge sheared into yielding flesh behind those big ears.

Leaving the head, Davy held the creature by the hind end and hastened on. When he came to where the sorrel had been hobbled, he slowly stood. He took it for granted that the animal had drifted, but it could not go far.

So where was it?

Davy turned from side to side. He was loath to accept that the horse was gone, yet he could not deny the obvious. The logical notion was that the war party had found it. Once again Providence had dashed a fleeting hope. Now he was

73

stuck afoot with the two females to protect, an unappealing proposition if ever there was one.

The Irishman faced the west. He knew where other horses were, horses that were heavily guarded, horses no one in his right mind would contemplate going after, but horses for the taking if someone was clever enough. When a man found himself between a rock and a hard place, he had to choose the lesser of two evils.

Loosening his belt, he shoved the rabbit partially under it, then drew the buckle snug. He would need both hands free.

The wind picked up again, as it did every night, but this time Davy did not mind. Any movement of the grass would be blamed on it. Pulling his coonskin cap lower, he headed for the Indian camp. The horses had been tethered on the north side, but by now they were probably in the middle, surrounded by the warriors. Slipping in and snatching one would be difficult.

Every ten strides he stopped to reconnoiter. Seven or eight horses, no matter how well restrained, inevitably made noise. A nicker, the stomp of a hoof, the swish of a tail, *something* was bound to give their presence away.

Davy guessed that he was within forty feet of where the camp had been when he smelled a lingering whiff of smoke. For the longest while he lay rock-still, listening. Frowning, he finally rose and walked to where smoldering embers sparked red. So much for getting his hands on a horse. The Indians had gone. Pivoting, he surveyed the darkling expanse.

Where to?

A possibility dawned on him, a horrible possibility that set him racing southward as if the hounds of hell nipped at his heels. In his mind echoed the names of those who might pay for his stupidity with their lives.

Heather and Becky!

*   *   *

Flavius Harris dreamed again.

Matilda had just plowed the south forty and was fixing supper. At his bidding, she came out onto the porch to massage his sore shoulders. He had spent the whole day in his rocking chair, and was stiff from lack of exercise.

Life was grand. Matilda had been waiting on him hand and foot since he returned. Why, she even scrubbed his back when he risked his health by taking a bath.

"I've missed you so much, my dearest beloved."

Flavius grinned, then saw her cat approaching. Times past, she'd doted on that calico critter as if it were a long-lost child. She even preferred it to him in bed. Claimed that it kept her warmer. Now his grin widened and he drew back his left foot. "I've been meaning to do this for years."

"Do what, handsome?"

"Take a gander." Flavius shoved the feline clear off the porch. It landed on all fours, as cats are wont to do, arched its spine, and hissed at him like a den full of riled snakes. "I should shoot that ornery cuss," he observed, "and hang its mangy hide over the fireplace."

"Whatever you want, my darling, wonderful man."

Flavius bent forward a few more inches. "You're missing a spot. To the left and down a bit." She dutifully traced a nail to the spot and kneaded his skin. "Ahhhh. That's it. If'n I'd known you were so good at this, I'd have had you do it long ago."

Matilda just tittered gaily.

Flavius laughed when she pinched him. He did not laugh when she pinched him again, twice as hard. Nor did he find it humorous when she grabbed him by the hair and tugged. "What the hell?"

Belatedly, Flavius realized that the pain he was feeling was not part of his dream. It had drawn him out of his fantasy, into the world of the living. Once more someone pinched him, so hard that he flinched. And the pressure on his hair grew greater.

"Damn it all!"

Befuddled, drowsy, Flavius opened his eyes, and immediately wished he hadn't.

He was surrounded by painted warriors.

Chapter Six

Yet another brisk morning dawned. The squawk of a bird roused Davy Crockett. Sitting up, he shook his head to clear the cobwebs, then squinted at the rising sun. His stomach let him know that it did not appreciate going without food for nearly two days; it rumbled like thunder. Pressing his hands against the back of his head, he stretched, then glanced at the sleeping forms of Heather and Rebecca Dugan.

Davy had been thrilled to find they were safe and sound. Rather than wake them, he had hunkered and rested Liz across his thighs. Someone had to stay up all night keeping watch. But the best of intentions often run aground on the harsh rocks of reality. His weary body had refused to co-operate, and in the still hours before first light he had fallen asleep.

Now Davy scratched the stubble on his chin, adjusted his coonskin cap, and stood. Other than a flock of birds winging overhead and a coyote skulking to the northeast, the plain was devoid of life. Of the war party, of the horses, of Flavius, there was no trace.

A moan signaled that Heather was awake. She smacked her lips, scrunched her mouth, and patted her disheveled hair. "I feel like death warmed over," she mumbled.

"Shucks. You're as pretty as ever," Davy said. Being married twice had taught him that women had a knack for looking lovely in the morning, whereas men looked as if they had just taken a tumble from a high cliff and landed in a hog wallow.

"Flatterer," Heather said, grinning. The grin evaporated when Becky groaned and shifted and opened her eyes.

"Mother? Why is my head so fuzzy?"

Heather clasped her shoulders. "You've been sick. But praise the Lord! You've come out of it! At last!" She checked Becky's forehead and announced, "The fever hasn't broken yet, but you're not as hot as you were yesterday."

"A good sign," Davy admitted. Kneeling, he confirmed it. The worst of the sickness was over, though not the threat to the girl's life. To fully recover she required plenty of food, water, and rest. He could supply something to eat, but water and rest depended on circumstances over which he had no control. "How about breakfast?"

"You found something?" Heather asked.

Davy indicated the makeshift spit he had set up before dozing off. The rabbit had been neatly skinned and chopped into sizable chunks arranged on long, fragile branches pruned from the brush that lined the gulch. Soon he had flames crackling. He crouched on one side of the fire, Heather on the other, both of them staring at the juicy morsels like famished wolves.

"I won't even ask what it is," Heather commented.

Davy refrained from telling her. It might upset Becky, who was eyeing the meat as if it were manna from heaven.

"I'm thirsty," the girl said. "Is there anything to drink?"

"That's next," Davy promised—although how he would

make good on his pledge had him stumped. Their only recourse was to plod across the prairie until they stumbled on a waterway, and the child was in no condition for a long trek.

Heather was too impatient to wait. She snatched a small piece of meat off the end of the spit, rolled it in her palm, and blew on it. Like a starving bobcat she tore into the chunk with her front teeth. Tiny rivulets of blood trickled down her chin, but she did not mind. Manners were forgotten; society's rules were thrown out the window when a person was brought to the brink of extinction.

Peeling off a strip, Heather blew on it some more, then offered it to Becky. The girl weakly raised a hand to take it but could not hold her arm steady. So her mother fed her, one small piece at a time.

Davy tempered his own hunger until the meat was nice and brown. Helping himself to some, he ate slowly. To gulp it down would only make him sick. He handed a piece to Heather, who nibbled while feeding Becky. Without being obvious, he ate much less than they did.

Becky was smiling and had sat up under her own power before she was done. "That was the tastiest meal I've ever had, Mr. Crockett."

"As famished as we were, you'd say the same about fried worms."

Becky actually laughed. "No, I would not. No one eats worms."

The meal had done wonders to restore their spirits. Davy was averse to changing the subject, but precious daylight was being squandered. "I have a few things to say," he declared. "We're in a fix. Afoot, without provisions, hostile Indians to deal with, one of us feeling poorly, it's enough to give a body gray hairs." He playfully tweaked Becky's chin to give the impression that he was far less worried than he was. "But our plight isn't hopeless. There's a way out."

They hung on his every word.

"We need a horse. Ours have run off, and the only others to be had are the ones that belong to those warriors we tangled with."

"You're not suggesting that we steal theirs?" Heather asked, aghast.

"Not the war party's, no," Davy clarified. "They'll be on the lookout for us. What I propose is that we follow them, dog their tracks clear back to their village, and take what we need from the tribe's herd." He went on quickly to stifle her protest. "Usually it's the boys who keep watch, which will make it easier. Besides, they won't figure on us having the gall to pull such a stunt."

Davy did not mention that it would be a miracle if they reached the village alive. His object was to inspire hope, not crush it.

"But Becky can't walk—" Heather said.

"We'll take turns carrying her until she's strong enough to do it on her own." Davy tweaked the girl again. "It won't be a problem. A feather weighs more than she does."

They bought it, or at least Becky did. Heather had doubts she did not voice, but her expression reflected them. Davy took first turn toting Becky, who fell asleep with her cheek on his chest. They returned to the site of the war party's camp. From there, the hoofprints led to the southeast. Within a quarter of a mile he found where several of the warriors had dismounted and gone on ahead on foot. The tracks showed why.

"They have Flavius."

Now the trail bore to the southwest. The sorrel's prints stood out, since it was the only shod horse in the bunch. Davy walked briskly, invigorated by the meal and spurred by fear for his friend. The warriors had spared Heather and Becky, but they might not be so charitable toward Flavius.

He had been wrong about how light the child was. By midday his shoulders ached and his legs were sore, but he declined to give Becky to Heather when Heather asked, saying, "I'm not halfway winded yet. I'll let you know when it's your turn."

Most wild animals gave them a wide berth. Coyotes were common, as were deer that stayed well out of rifle range. At one point they came on a colony of prairie dogs. At a shrill whistle from a sentry, the creatures scampered into their dens. Later, Davy saw a large animal to the south, so large it had to be either a buffalo or a grizzly. Thankfully, whatever it was did not catch wind of them.

Shortly thereafter Heather insisted on carrying Becky. Davy stayed on the alert for something to shoot, but other than a curious hawk and several quail that were gone before he could bring Liz to bear, Nature did not oblige him.

"How far ahead do you think they are?" Heather inquired as the sun dipped and their shadows lengthened.

"Five or six hours," Davy admitted. By sundown tomorrow it would be twice as much. But so long as a storm did not wash away the tracks, time was not a factor.

Being so far behind was an advantage in one respect. Davy had no qualms about shooting an opossum that had no business being abroad before nightfall.

Heather regarded it with displeasure. "I've never eaten one of those things," she mentioned as he peeled the skin off with his tomahawk.

"Folks back home do all the time," Davy said. Backwoodsmen learned early on not to be too fussy about what they ate, not if they *wanted* to eat. He had fond recollections of the opossum dish his mother made. A favorite dish was fried strips garnished with onions and greens. "Do like my ma told me once. Hold your nose and close your eyes, and your stomach will be in for a big surprise."

Mother and daughter beamed. Despite being tired and grimy, despite the daunting challenge ahead, for the first time in days they were relaxed and relatively content. It pleased Davy no end. He finished butchering the opossum, his thoughts drifting to a much more serious matter.

"Why do you look so grim?" Heather asked.

"Flavius," Davy said simply.

"Don't worry. They haven't harmed him yet, have they? Maybe that means they intend to take him back to their village. He'll be safe until then."

Would he? Davy wondered. Or did the warriors have other plans?

At that exact moment, Flavius Harris was asking himself the same question. After a miserable day spent belly-down on the sorrel, his arms and legs bound, he had been dumped on the ground so hard that it set his head to ringing. The Indians had ignored him while they made camp. But seconds before one of the younger men had ambled over, sneered, and drawn a long knife from a beaded sheath.

Flavius tried to sit up. If he was to die, he would not do so meekly. He would not be helplessly slaughtered.

The warrior slammed a foot against his chest, knocking him flat. Again Flavius tried to sit, but the man pressed down, pinning him, then bent and stuck the tip of the blade against the base of his throat.

This was it! Flavius feared. He was going to have his jugular slit. At least there would not be much pain. He grit his teeth to keep them from shaking, and wished Davy could be there to see how well he died.

To his astonishment, the warrior reached lower and pried at the knots on the rope that bound his wrists. Soon his hands were free. Smirking, the Indian jabbed his neck, pricking the skin. It hurt, but Flavius did not flinch.

Straightening, the warrior touched a finger to the tiny drop of blood on the blade, then rubbed the fingertip on both cheeks, smearing thin red lines. Then the man sheathed the weapon and walked off.

What was that all about? Flavius thought as he gingerly ran a hand over his throat, verifying that the cut was small and not very deep. His forearms were partially numb from having been tied so long, so he flexed his fingers and wriggled his wrists to restore circulation.

The Indians showed no interest in him whatsoever. Shortly before they had halted, one had downed a buck with an arrow. Several were carving it up.

Since they had freed his hands, Flavius took it for granted that they would not object if he untied his legs. Bending, he tugged at a knot. A savage cry burst from a nearby warrior, and suddenly two of them were beside him with knives drawn. Flavius jerked both hands overhead and blurted, "Sorry! I figured it would be all right."

Glaring, the pair backed off. Flavius exhaled in relief that was short-lived. Another warrior, a stately man whose long hair bore gray streaks, came toward him. This one had an air of authority about him. Flavius had noticed that the others treated him with deference and appeared to readily do his bidding. Plainly, the man was the leader of the war party. Maybe even a tribal chief.

Mustering a smile, Flavius said, "Howdy, mister. I sure hope you're not one of those who hate whites just because our skin color's different."

The elderly warrior scrutinized him, saying nothing.

"Do you speak the white man's tongue?" Flavius asked. The warrior kept on studying him as if he were a type of critter never seen before. "How about the Creek language?" Flavius had learned a smattering during the war, enough to ask for food when his company visited the villages of friendly Creeks. "I am a friend," he declared in the Creek tongue, garnering no response.

Inspiration motivated Flavius to hold his right hand in front of his neck with the palm out, his index and second fingers pointed straight up. He raised the hand until it was level with his head, then looked expectantly at the warrior.

Some time ago, Davy had been taken prisoner by the Nadowessioux, as the French called them, or Sioux, as they were more commonly known. During his captivity, Davy had learned many of the peculiar hand signs the Sioux and other tribes used. Davy had offered to teach them all to Flavius, but Flavius had only bothered to memorize a few. One of those was the sign for "friend," which he had just made.

The elderly warrior acted surprised. His hands flew in a series of signs, too many and too rapidly for Flavius to comprehend. When the warrior was done, Flavius shook his head and shrugged.

The warrior's brow furrowed. Turning, he pointed at the body of the man slain by Heather, then at Flavius, and made more hand talk, none of which Flavius understood. But he gathered that the warrior did not accept his assertion of friendship, that the proof lay wrapped in the bloody blanket. It was the warrior's turn to gaze down expectantly. Flavius was at a loss. None of the few signs he had learned could possibly explain how the death had come about. In any event, his captors would not take kindly to learning that Davy and he meant only to steal a few horses.

The elderly warrior returned to the fire. Flavius leaned back, dejected. Where was Davy, anyhow? What could have happened to him? Why hadn't he shown up to help? Initially, Flavius had been afraid the war party had made buzzard bait of his friend. But if that had been the case, the warriors would have helped themselves to Davy's guns and tomahawk and personal effects.

So, apparently, Davy had gotten away. And a fat lot of good that did Flavius. Davy did not have a horse, and was further burdened by Heather and Becky. Flavius could forget about his friend coming to his rescue. The only one who could get him out of the fix he was in was himself, a discouraging notion.

Flavius held no illusions about his ability. He did not think fast on his feet, like Davy. Nor was he anywhere near as clever, or half as strong. Truth was, without Davy he'd have been dead a dozen times over. Now, on his own, his prospects were as slim as a blade of grass.

The Indians were roasting their supper. They were subdued, speaking in low tones. Occasional glances cast in his direction were hardly friendly.

The dead man had been placed a goodly distance from the fire. During the day Flavius had observed that they tended to shy away from it. Some tribes, he'd heard tell, believed it was bad medicine to be near a dead person. Perhaps these fellows were the same.

To his great surprise, the elderly warrior walked over bearing a large piece of meat. Without comment the man plopped it in Flavius's lap and wheeled. "I'm obliged," Flavius exclaimed. Famished, he held the piece under his nose to savor the aroma. His natural impulse was to devour it in three gulps, but he willed himself to go slowly and finished about the same time the warriors did. Plenty of meat was left, meat that was cut into strips and placed on a flat rock close to the fire to dry.

Darkness was descending.

Flavius mulled an escape attempt. Once the warriors turned in, he would try to sneak past them to the horses. The saddle had been stripped from the sorrel, but he could ride bareback if need be. He would head due east until he struck the Mississippi, then go south to St. Louis.

His scheme was spoiled by the same young warrior who had pricked his neck. The man materialized out of nowhere, roughly shoved him flat, and tightly bound his wrists. As an added insult, the warrior poked his ribs a few times. Snickering, the man left him.

Flavius did not sit back up. Why should he bother? His fate was sealed. The Indians would take him to their village and torture him to death. No one would ever know how he met his end. Davy, Matilda, his close friends and kin, they'd go to their graves wondering. Would any of them shed a tear? Matilda, perhaps. Davy, maybe.

He felt like shedding some himself.

* * *

"You should be asleep, like your mother."

Rebecca Dugan sighed and shifted. She was on her side next to Heather, who had been slumbering for the better part of an hour. Becky, however, could not stop fidgeting and squirming. Now she rose onto an elbow, whispering, "Don't think I haven't been trying. I just can't. I'm sorry."

Davy was across the fire, his legs bent under him, Liz across his thighs. "Want more possum?"

"Goodness gracious, no. I'm stuffed." Becky patted her belly and giggled. "I haven't eaten that much in my whole life."

"I take it you're not as fussy about eating possum as your ma is?"

"It was greasy, but tasty. I wonder why they don't serve it at public eating places. I never saw it on a menu."

Davy grinned. "Been to a good many, have you?"

"Sure. My grandfather took us out to eat a lot. To his private club. To inns. To taverns. To an eating house down by the wharves. All over."

"You're a regular lady of the world, aren't you?"

"What does that mean?"

"You've been all over, seen a lot of sights."

"Not that many. I'm not even twelve yet. I have a long way to go before I'm a lady."

The wavering howl of a wolf briefly intruded. "Being a lady has nothing to do with how old you are," Davy said. "It has to do with how you are inside." He paused. "What if I was to tell you that you've been to more fancy eating places than both of my wives combined?"

"You're joshing."

"Not hardly. We never had money to spare for frivolities. The little I make goes for essentials like ammunition and shoes for the kids and flour and dry goods."

Becky propped her chin in a hand. "What do you do for a living, Mr. Crockett? I don't believe you ever told us."

"I hunt."

"That's all?"

"Living in the backwoods isn't like living in the big city, girl. We don't have folks waiting on us hand and foot. We have to make ends meet as best we can." Davy leaned back. "People where I come from grow their own food, make their own clothes, tend themselves when they're sick." An image of Elizabeth shimmered in his mind's eye. "My wife tills our garden and sews and knits, and she's darn skilled at it, too. Me, I keep food on the table. Twelve months of the year, day in and day out, I make sure my family doesn't starve. That's a heap of a responsibility."

"How do you make any money at it?"

"I don't like to crow about myself, but I'm one of the best bear hunters in all of Tennessee. I earn a few dollars here and there by helping other men lay away bear meat for the winter. I sell pelts, too, mainly bear and coon. Wolf hides, sometimes, but they're a lot harder to come by."

"Do you like to kill?"

It was the type of brutally blunt question that only someone of her tender years would broach. "Whether I like it or not's got nothing to do with it. My family has to eat, and in order to feed them, I have to kill game." She did not appear satisfied, so Davy elaborated. "I've been doing it since I was knee-high to a praying mantis. It comes as naturally to me as breathing or sleeping."

"But doesn't it upset you? Killing an innocent animal, I mean?"

"Innocent how? In case you hadn't noticed, practically every living creature kills to survive. Insects feed on plants and other insects, birds and fish feed on the insects, mammals feed on the birds and fish, and we feed on the whole kit and caboodle." The wolf howled again, closer. "That's one of the gripes I have about cities. They tend to make people forget how the world works. City-bred folks think that being waited on hand and foot is the natural order of things, when the real way of the world is dog eat dog."

87

"You make cities sound bad."

"In a way, they are. Have you ever held a broken piece of glass up to the light? It distorts everything. Cities are like that glass. They give us a false notion of how things are. And how can we be true to ourselves if we can't be true to what's around us?"

Becky was growing drowsy. Yawning, she said, "You have me all confused. Me, I like city life. It's real peaceful. No one is trying to kill you. No wild animals are out to rip you to bits. I feel safe in a city. I don't out here."

She had a valid point, but Davy pressed his argument. "Cities aren't the havens you make them out to be. They breed human vermin like murderers, cheats, and liars. Not to mention politicians."

"So are you saying there shouldn't be any cities or towns? That we'd all be better off if we lived in the country?" Her eyelids fluttered, and she yawned again. "I may not be very smart, but that strikes me as silly."

"Me too, I reckon," Davy admitted. "Now, why don't you lie down and get some more rest. We have another long day ahead of us tomorrow."

"You won't need to carry me. I can walk just fine."

"Fibber. You're too weak yet. We'll carry you until you can outrun an antelope."

She giggled. "No one can do that. You'll be carrying me until I'm old and wrinkly." Lowering to the ground, she cupped her cheek on her hand and added dreamily, "I like you, Mr. Crockett. Thank you for all you've done for us."

"Anytime."

Rebecca fell silent and within moments was breathing heavily. Heather had not moved once. Davy took the liberty of building the fire up a smidgen to keep them warm. He heard the wolf again, closer than ever. To the southeast a blazing greenish light flashed through the sky. A meteor, he figured. As he followed its arc to the horizon, he saw a pair of slanted red orbs peering at him from the darkness. Swiveling, he discovered more, dozens of disembodied eyes fixed on the camp. It was downright spooky.

A low growl identified the owners of those eyes. One set glided nearer. Out of the inky blackness the shape of a wolf solidified, a large beast with an unusual white spot on its chest. The animal stopped and looked at Heather and Becky.

Davy brought the rifle to his shoulder. Wolves were not particularly ferocious; none had ever attacked him, anyway. If these did, he could not drop them all. Maybe two or three. With any luck the rest would turn tail.

The wolf with the white spot uttered a strange whine. Rotating, it padded off into the nocturnal domain that had spawned it. As if that were a signal, the rest of the pack melted into the night, living specters, there one instant, gone the next.

The Irishman did not lower his gun until a wail in the distance assured him it was safe. Or as safe as it could be with the prairie crawling with wolves, bears, and big cats.

Becky had hit the nail on the head. As much as he loved the wilderness, Davy had to concede that it was no place for people like the Dugans. They were as out of place as catfish on dry land. City folk were like pampered pets. They had to be led around by a leash and hand-fed, or they couldn't cope.

It troubled Davy to think that he had more in common with that pack of wolves than he did with most of the human race. For as long as he lived, he would never take to wearing a collar. Being coddled stripped a man of his dignity. It robbed an individual of the one crucial gift bestowed by genuine freedom: being self-sufficient.

Give me freedom or give me death, Davy mused, and smiled. The sentiment was hardly original, but it was one he would live by until they planted him in his grave.

Chapter Seven

After seven days of grueling travel Flavius Harris stopped counting. The days tended to blur, one into another, so that it seemed to him as if his life had become an endless bone-numbing routine of constant misery. Each day was exactly like the one before it, a grueling pattern cut from the same torturous cloth.

Flavius's day always started with his being roughly snapped out of fitful sleep by strong hands that threw him over the sorrel. Ten hours of riding on his belly ensued, gut-wrenching hours that left him sore and stiff and nursing a knot of pain in his abdomen. Usually his captors allowed him half an hour in which to eat. Barely would his arms and hands return to normal before he was bound again. Each long, anxious night was spent curled into a ball on the damp ground, with no blanket for warmth. Every morning, toward dawn, the cold would cut into him like an icy knife. It would set his teeth to chattering, his body to quaking violently.

Day after day after day was the same; night after night

after night Flavius pined for Tennessee and lamented his misspent life. That it was coming to a close, that the final chapter in his earthly odyssey was about to be written, he had no doubt. As soon as the war party reached their village, his fate would be sealed. A grisly, horrible fate, the kind he once liked to talk about over his cups among friends at the tavern, the kind that happened to *other* people, the sort that set a man's neck to prickling and gave him nightmares. Such as the massacre at Fort Mims by the Creeks, or the time a farmer named Johnson was found mutilated, his eyes gouged out, his tongue chopped off, and, oddly, every other finger and toe missing.

Flavius tried to steel himself for the inevitable. He did not lack for bravery, but he was honestly uncertain whether he could endure prolonged torment without crying out, without betraying his manhood and bringing shame to the Harris name. So what if he was the only one who would know? It was enough. He would fade into eternity tainted by humiliation. The sole saving grace would be that his father and brothers were not there to see him besmirch the family reputation.

Smothered by despair, Flavius lost track of the hours, of the days, of the nights. So he was all the more surprised when, one sunny afternoon, he heard the tinkle of childish laughter and dogs barking. Rousing himself, he lifted his head and saw a village ahead—more lodges than he could count, a great village, the Indian equivalent of St. Louis or New Orleans.

A cloud of dust to one side merited his interest. Under it milled thousands of horses, more horses than he had ever seen in one place at one time, more horses than logic dictated the tribe would ever need. *Whoever these Indians are, they're powerfully fond of the critters*, he reflected.

It was to be expected. During the long journey, Flavius had witnessed the skill of those who captured him. For amusement they often urged their animals into a gallop and put on an exhibition the likes of which would astound most European riding masters. Their horsemanship was without peer.

With amazing agility, they could ride at full speed and swing onto the off side of their mounts so that only an ankle and part of a hand were visible, rendering them impossible to hit in battle. They knew acrobatic tricks that dazzled the brain. Whirling and twirling with remarkable skill, they scorned gravity.

Despite himself, Flavius had been impressed. They had a very special relationship with their horses, these Indians. And their animals were worthy of the devotion. For as Flavius learned more about the warhorses, as he learned their character and daily observed how they behaved, he learned that they were some of the finest anywhere. They possessed all the qualities a man looked for in a mount: alertness, swiftness, endurance, and intelligence.

As an uncle of his had been so fond of saying, animals did not grow on trees. They had to be selectively bred, the bad strains culled, the superior bloodlines improved—clearly a principle these Indians practiced. They were first-rate horse breeders, the presence of the enormous herd testifying to how seriously they applied themselves.

Flavius's study of the herd was cut short. Suddenly he found himself the focus of intense scrutiny. Women and children thronged around, each eager for a peek. The smallest timidly hung back, but the older boys and girls and the women pressed in close, poking and jostling him.

One white-haired matron went so far as to grab his hair, yank his head up, and pry at his lips with a gnarled finger. It startled him so badly that he did not resist. She gouged a nail against his gums, then ran a finger over his upper and lower teeth, grunted, and gave a curt nod.

Flavius laughed aloud. Damn him if the old biddy hadn't examined him as if he were a horse! Checking if he was healthy! But what difference did it make, when they intended to kill him eventually? As that same uncle had also liked to say, there was no explaining heathens. They were as unpredictable as the weather, as temperamental as a hurricane. "They're just not like us God-fearing folk," the uncle frequently declared.

Flavius knew that Davy claimed the two peoples were a lot more alike than either was willing to admit. That the white man and the red man could live in peace, if they'd sincerely try. That there was no need for the endless bloodshed. But then, Davy Crockett was probably the only white man in all of Tennessee who felt it was wrong for the government to forcibly relocate Indians from their homelands to make room for more settlers.

It was the Irishman's one true failing, his soft spot, as it were. And all because some Indians once saved his life.

Flavius could understand being grateful. If it had happened to him, he would have given the Indians a horse, or maybe a couple of blankets and a handful of trinkets. That was how it was done. Indians loved trinkets. Everyone knew that. They'd have gone their merry way, content, and he would have gotten on with his life, just as it was before.

But no, not Crockett! Davy had to go around befriending *all* Indians. As if he had to repay the kindness done him a million times over. It made no blamed sense.

The sorrel came to a halt. The war party had reached the center of the great circle and the warriors were dismounting. Flavius, licking his parched lips, twisted to try to see what was going on. If the savages were going to make wolf meat of him right away, he'd like to know. For the moment, though, they ignored him. A stocky warrior dressed in the finest of buckskins had arrived—a high chief, judging by the attitude of the people. The newcomer stood before the horse bearing the corpse of the man slain by Heather, and bowed his head.

The body had begun to stink long before. Instead of burying it, the war party had bundled it in layers of deer hide, adding more and more layers as time went by until it resembled a bloated sausage. It stank worse and worse as time went on, yet they would not get rid of it.

A shriek rent the village. From out of the crowd hurtled a woman who tried to throw herself at the corpse. Timely intervention stopped her. Kicking and wailing, she was dragged from the scene. In her wake, the assemblage fell totally silent. It was so quiet that Flavius could hear a fly buzz.

All eyes swung toward him. Flavius wanted to wilt—to wither away to nothingness, or to sink into the ground and keep on sinking until he came out in China. Swallowing to moisten his raw throat, he croaked, "It wasn't me. I'm not to blame. Do any of you savvy?"

No one responded. The stocky warrior issued instructions. The tall warrior who had led the war party personally guided the sorrel to a nearby lodge. All the dwellings were constructed of high poles and cured buffalo hides, similar to those of the Sioux described by Davy. Paintings on the outer surfaces were common, though what they signified was a mystery.

A pair of young warriors dumped Flavius on the ground. His shoulder spiked with a severe pain, and he lay still to recover. They denied him the luxury. He was roughly hauled erect and shoved into the lodge. He had to stoop to get through the doorway, and, stumbling, he drew up short.

The interior was neat and clean, not the hovel Flavius had anticipated. Overhead was an airhole—for ventilation, he reckoned. Since he was a condemned prisoner, he had not counted on having company. But he did—a young woman and an old woman were on their knees to one side. "How-do, ladies," he blurted.

The older woman rose. In the gloom it took Flavius a few seconds to realize that she was the same white-haired crone who had examined his teeth. She was partial to a long stick she used for a cane. Hobbling over, she warily circled him, as someone might a rabid dog.

It would be smart to gain a friend, Flavius decided. Smiling, he said, "I'm right pleased to make your acquaintance, ma'am. There's been a terrible misunderstanding. We never meant to get in a scrape with your warriors. Honest Injun. You see, we were—"

The cane whizzed, striking Flavius across the shins. Yelping, he toppled, in so much pain that he could barely think straight. "Why'd you do that, you miserable witch?" he bawled. "I ain't out to harm you."

Again the woman struck, across the shoulders. To spare himself further anguish, Flavius tried to crawl into a corner. Only, there were no corners. The lodge was circular. Compensating, he backed against a pile of blankets and grabbed one for a shield.

The old woman had followed, the cane raised to wallop the tar out of him. It was a word from the younger woman that saved him. Huffing, the old one backed off, but she wagged her walking stick menacingly.

Flavius rested his head on the blankets, hugged the one he held, and fought back a wave of tears. He'd not had a good long cry in ages; he was long overdue. It wasn't manly, true, but a man could endure only so much. A single tear trickled from his left eye. He was on the brink of a deluge when the old woman did the one thing she could do that would stiffen his resolve.

She laughed.

Flavius looked up. The crone jabbed her cane at his cheek and mewed like a kitten—or like a baby whining for its mother's milk. The younger woman motioned at her, but the old one kept on laughing and pointing. Furious at the insult, Flavius clamped his jaw shut and refused to shed another drop. He would be damned if he'd give her the satisfaction.

The old witch said something. Flavius refused to face them, refused to have anything else to do with anyone in the whole tribe. He was inspired by newfound determination. He had tapped into a vein of iron will, and his emotions were under complete control. Nothing could make him acknowledge their existence.

Then his stomach rumbled.

"Water," Becky Dugan rasped. "Please. We need water."

No one knew that better than Davy Crockett. It was their second day without, and he was thirsty enough to drink any of the Great Lakes dry.

All had gone well until a few mornings before. Each evening he had brought down an animal for their supper. Each dawn they had gathered enough dew to slake their thirst. Then game grew scarce, and although Davy roamed farther afield than ever, farther than was safe, he failed to find food. At the same time, the mornings grew warmer, reducing the amount of dew to practically nothing.

Now two days had elapsed, two whole days with no nourishment whatsoever. Davy carried Becky. She was able to walk if need be, but she was not up to snuff. As for Heather, the woman had been pushed past the limits of her endurance. Exhaustion etched her once lovely features, bags sagged under her once magnificent eyes. Her clothes were soiled, the hem tattered, her shoes in disrepair.

They're on their last legs, Davy mused. Unless Providence intervened, their time left on earth could be measured in hours, not weeks. Mechanically, he plodded to the southwest. Why he continued to do so when any hope of saving Flavius was gone, why he persisted when starvation loomed and death was imminent, he couldn't say. Habit, maybe. Once a Crockett set out to do something, he saw it through. Come what may.

It was late afternoon. Dimly, Dave felt a warm breeze caress the stubble that dotted his chin. He was in sore need of a shave and a bath, not to mention a solid week of rest in bed.

Thinking about Elizabeth helped take his mind off his woes. Thinking of the many cozy nights spent snuggling, of the socials they attended. She loved to mix and mingle, and she had a passion for dancing. Secretly, so did he. He'd never fess up to it in front of his friends for fear of being teased. Men weren't supposed to *like* to dance.

What of his brood? How were they faring? He'd had three kids by his first wife, poor Polly. Elizabeth already had two of her own when they hitched up, and she wanted to have another three or four before she was past her childbearing prime. Once, he'd joked that at the rate he was going, he'd have enough to start his own school and set himself up as the teacher. Wouldn't that be a hell of a note?

Suddenly a creature appeared in the distance. Stopping, Davy squinted to make it out, but it was distorted by the haze. The size suggested a deer or antelope, maybe something bigger. "Game," he croaked, and sat Becky down. "Stay put," he told them.

Heather merely nodded. She had taken to having long spells of moody quiet. Late at night, sometimes, she sobbed softly with her face buried in her arms.

"I won't be long," Davy promised. It hurt his parched throat to speak. Hefting Liz, he stalked toward the figure. Now figures. Several had appeared and were bunched together. The range was much too great, but he fixed a bead on them anyway, not really intending to shoot. To his consternation, they trotted to the south a couple of dozen yards. Then they vanished, in the snap of a finger.

That can't be, Davy told himself. Mentally reaching into the tiny reservoir of stamina he had not yet tapped, he ran toward the spot. To clear his head, he slapped both cheeks. Hard. Odds were he'd get off only one shot, so he had to make it count.

Antelope normally bolted before a hunter came anywhere

near them. So when none showed themselves, Davy suspected he had stumbled on deer. For once things were going his way. He smiled when he spied a wash ahead. Flattening, he crawled to the rim and cautiously poked his head out so as not to scare the deer into bounding off.

Four horses stood at rest at the bottom. Four horses fitted with saddles and saddlebags and water skins.

Saddles? Water skins! Davy pushed onto his knees and threw back his head to whoop for joy. The riders were white! Heather and Becky and he were saved!

Footsteps pounded to his rear. Davy started to turn, but husky bodies slammed into his back and he was smashed to the ground. Liz was ripped from his grasp. Whoever had pounced on him spun him around and hoisted him to his feet. Two brawny frontiersmen had hold of both arms, and two more were in front. They were as dark as Indians, their hides bronzed by ceaseless exposure to the sun, but there was no denying that they were white. Davy smiled broadly, so overcome with relief and joy that words failed him.

A strapping young frontiersman took a step closer. He wore an unusual wide-brimmed black hat and sported fancy ivory-handled flintlocks wedged under a wide studded belt. "Why's this jasper grinning like an idiot?"

A man with gray streaks at the temples and a sober air shook his head. "I ain't rightly sure, Farley. Maybe he's one of them there scatterbrains. They say that Injuns won't harm simpletons."

One of the men holding Davy, a black-haired rogue whose left cheek bore a jagged scar, said thickly, "Simpleton, hell. It's an act, Taylor. He's one of the filthy vermin who been tradin' with the Comanches. I say we stake him out over an anthill, like those red bastards did to my cousin."

"Simmer down, Kerr," Taylor said. "We ain't about to send a man to meet his Maker 'less'n we have proof he deserves it."

Kerr was a sulky bear whose glower would frighten children. "Proof be damned! Why else is he out here in the heart of Comanche country all by his lonesome? He must have his pack animals hid somewheres. Let's stake him out, then go find 'em."

Taylor shook his head. "You're putting the cart before the horse."

"That's right," Farley said. "It's only fair this feller gets to speak his piece." Nodding at Davy, he declared, "Cat got your tongue, mister? Who are you? What are you doing here?"

Nothing would please the Irishman more than to answer. But his mouth and throat were so dry that the only sounds he could utter were strangled syllables.

"See? A simpleton," Taylor said. "All he can talk is gibberish."

"It's an act," Kerr insisted.

The fourth frontiersman sided with Taylor. "I don't know. Look at his eyes. And how his mouth keeps a-twitching. He appears awful addlepated to me. Reminds me of that hog I had to shoot when it went mad." He shuddered and slackened his grip. "Makes my skin crawl. What if it's catching?"

Davy found his voice at last. "I'm no damn simpleton!" he rasped, tearing his right arm loose. "And I ain't been wolf-bit! What I am is lost and hungry and thirsty!"

"Lost?" Taylor repeated. "How could a grown man get lost out here?" He motioned at the unending sea of grass, then at the blue vault above. "The sun rises in the east and sets in the west. What's hard to figure out about that?"

"No, no," Davy said. "I'm not *lost* lost—"

"What did I tell you?" the fourth man said. "Addlepated."

Davy tried to pry Kerr's fingers off, but the scarred malcontent squeezed harder. "Let go of me," Davy insisted. "The others need water and food. Go help them, then I'll explain everything. Please."

"Others?" Taylor said.

Farley started to pivot. "What others?"

The click of a pistol hammer being cocked riveted everyone in place. "Release him," Heather Dugan said flatly, "or so help me, I'll put a ball smack between your eyes." She had come up on them unnoticed, Becky behind her, the pistol Davy had lent her held steady in her right hand. She was addressing Kerr, who took one look at the muzzle of the smoothbore and immediately backed off several strides, raising his hands.

"Hold on there, lady. Be careful with that thing. I'm not hankerin' to be killed by accident."

Heather shifted so she had a clear shot at all four. "I assure you that if I do pull this trigger, there will be nothing accidental about it." The others were so stupefied by her arrival that they gaped in bewilderment. Wagging the pistol to shoo them to one side, Heather sidled toward the Tennessean. "Did they hurt you?"

The last thing on Davy's mind were the bruises he had sustained. "They have water," he said, nodding at the wash. "They do?"

Heather and Becky both licked their lips, and Becky wriggled in protest, bleating, "Hurry! If I don't get something to drink soon, I'll faint."

Davy snatched his rifle from Taylor and covered the quartet. "Go help yourselves," he instructed mother and daughter. "I'll watch these coons." Backing off, he tried not to dwell on those full skins beaded with moisture. *Oh, for a sweet taste!* His tongue felt swollen, his throat was a desert.

Farley regained his wits first. "Sorry, mister. We didn't realize you had your wife and daughter along or we'd've known you couldn't be a gunrunner."

"That's right," Taylor concurred. "You have to understand our position. Desperate times call for desperate measures. So many lives have been lost that we're apt to shoot first and ask questions second."

Davy's temples drummed from the pounding he had taken.

Their jabber only made his condition worse. Gesturing sharply, he snapped, "Hush. We'll set things straight directly."

"You seem to be feeling poorly," Taylor said. "Is there anything we can do?"

"Poorly is an understatement," Davy allowed. Dampening his lips, he inquired, "Where are you boys from, anyhow?"

"We hail from down San Antonio way," Farley answered.

"Where?"

"San Antonio de Bexar," Farley amended.

"Never heard of it," Davy admitted. "But I've yet to set foot in Missouri."

Farley and Taylor exchanged looks. "Missouri?" Farley said. "Don't they have maps where you hail from?"

"We're Texians," Taylor explained.

Astonishment befuddled Davy. "Texas? Isn't that a province of Mexico? What in blue blazes are you gents doing so far from home?"

"Us?" Taylor said, then squinted upward. To his friends he said, "It must be the heat. The sun fried his brain and he's not thinking straight." Taylor smiled at the Irishman and encompassed the prairie with a grand sweep. "Begging your pardon, friend. But where do you think you are? You're *in* Texas."

"North Texas, to be exact," Farley said.

A feather could have bowled Davy over. He gawked in dazed disbelief, exclaiming, "It can't be!" Surely he'd have known, he told himself. Mulling it over, though, he realized he was being foolish. No signs were posted in the middle of the wasteland, no markers to signify the boundary between the land claimed by the United States and that under the control of its neighbor to the south.

Kerr was amused by his confusion. "This here is Comanche land," he said, accenting each word, much as an adult might to a child who could not master basic geography. "At least, they claim it is. We've been scrappin with 'em for years now, but so far they've had the upper hand.''

The fourth man nodded. "That's right, stranger. They raid us to their heart's content. Hardly a week goes by that a cabin isn't burned, or cattle run off, or someone's taken captive. They're devils. Coldhearted animals. Every last one of 'em deserves to be exterminated.''

"Texas?" Davy said. He just could not get over it. Back in Tennessee he'd dallied with the notion of one day taking a gallivant down that way, just as he did of one day traveling to the Pacific Ocean, maybe visiting California and the Oregon country. But they were dreams. Fervent wishes he never saw coming to pass.

"Where are you from?" Taylor asked.

Davy answered, adding, "My pard's in the clutches of a band I've been trailing for the better part of a month. I never did learn who they were, but it must be those Comanches you're so wrought up about.''

"Do tell," Taylor said. "Then I propose we join forces.''

Farley pushed his wide-brimmed hat back on his head and hooked his thumbs in his belt. "A year ago, my sister and a cousin were stolen. We had no idea who was to blame until recently. Two Claws is his name, and his village is in this area. We aim to take the women back or die in the attempt.''

Frankly phrased, bravely stated. First impressions were always important to Davy. He liked the brash young Texian and sympathized with Farley's plight, but he had another problem besides Flavius. "I'd be happy to oblige, but I can't put Mrs. Dugan and her daughter in any more danger. They've been through pure hell, boys, and that's the gospel.''

Farley glanced at the wash. "Mrs. Dugan? She's not your wife?''

"A widow. She lost her man to the Pawnees.'' Davy saw fit not to mention all the details. The Texians might hold what he had done to Alexander Dugan against him. "We

103

were trying to reach St. Louis when the Comanches got ahold of my partner.''

At that juncture Heather and Rebecca traipsed up out of the wash, Heather with a water skin. They were smiling, happy, refreshed. Their faces glistened, their hair was drenched, the tops of their dresses were soaked.

Farley stood as one mesmerized, declaring under his breath, ''My word, but she's beautiful.''

''That she is,'' Kerr agreed.

Davy lowered his rifle. The only danger the Texians posed was of an amorous nature. With their help, he just might rescue his friend yet. Gratefully, he accepted the skin and drank greedily, but not so greedily that he became sick.

At long last his luck had turned.

Now all he could do was pray that Flavius was still alive.

Chapter Eight

Flavius Harris slept as soundly as a baby his first night in the village, much to his surprise. He was at a loss to explain why. Maybe it was having a roof over his head for the first time in months, even if it was a hide roof and not the roughly hewn beams of a log cabin. Maybe it was the meal the old crone fed him that evening, a delicious stew laced with chunks of buffalo meat and wild onions. Or maybe being so cozy was the reason; the fire kept him toasty the whole night through. It was almost enough to make him thankful he was a captive.

For once, Flavius awoke refreshed. He stretched, and smiled, and patted his stomach, wondering what tasty breakfast the old woman would serve. The whistle of her cane slicing the air was the only forewarning he had that he had earned her displeasure. It caught him on the left forearm, eliciting so much torment that he doubled over, pressing the arm against his stomach. "What the blazes was that for?" he hollered, glancing up.

The white-haired fury had raised the cane for another swing. She snapped at him in her language, then pointed at the entrance. The flap hung open. Sunlight streamed inside, revealing that it was well past dawn.

Was she mad because he had overslept? Flavius took a lesson from his coon dogs and groveled at her feet, saying, ''I'm sorry!'' When another blow was not forthcoming, he timidly looked up. She was outside, beckoning.

Casting the blanket off, Flavius scrambled out into the glare of sunshine. He squinted in order to see. The village was going about its daily routine. Children played. Men sharpened knives and fixed bows and crafted lances. Women were engaged in a variety of tasks, from curing hides to sewing to drying meat. The latter made his mouth water.

A mild hit on the leg reminded him not to let his thoughts stray. The old woman pointed at a pair of large jugs, then at him. Comprehending, he picked them up and dutifully followed her northward. The warriors and other women generally ignored him, but the children were fascinated. Many ran in close to touch or poke him, some using sharpened sticks. When one poked too hard, he paused to glare at the culprit.

A swish of the cane heralded intense pain in his temple. Flavius nearly fell. His vision spun and his knees were briefly wobbly.

Spitting commands, the crone gestured for him to keep going.

Bowing meekly, Flavius obeyed. The boy who had poked him and some of the others laughed, and were brazen enough to pester him repeatedly until he came to the last of the lodges. As if by magic, the children abruptly peeled away.

A hundred yards off gurgled a wide stream. Flavius did not have to be told what to do. Unbidden, he filled the two jugs. They were now so heavy that he had to struggle to lift them, and he tottered as he walked. He was on the lookout for the children, afraid they would renew their assault once he entered the village. But they stayed away.

The old woman had him deposit the jugs in her lodge. Tired, Flavius sat, and just as promptly jumped up when she hit him across the shoulders. The jugs were but the first of many chores she had for him to do, chores that did not allow for a moment's rest from sunrise to sunset. He hauled water for half the lodges in the village, he gathered dried buffalo droppings to use as fuel for fires, he collected firewood from a stand of cottonwoods to the northeast, he helped to skin two white-tailed deer, he carried heavy parfleches. It was safe to say that Flavius had never worked so hard any one day in his whole life.

When the crone finally ushered him to her lodge and indicated that he should lie in his usual spot, Flavius was so relieved, he grabbed her hand and kissed the withered skin over her knuckles. It was a token of his appreciation, but she misconstrued. Yelping, she belabored him with the cane, desisting only when he curled into a ball with a blanket over him for protection.

Muttering loudly, the woman walked off. Flavius, rubbing his shoulder, peeked out and saw her leave. He was alone for the first time since they brought him to the village. But he could not enjoy it much. His muscles ached, his sinews were sore, several of his joints bothered him, and his lower back was a mass of pain.

"I'm still alive, though," Flavius said aloud. It was something. Hell, it was *everything*.

For how much longer was the issue. He had helped ready a large lodge for a council to be held later on. No doubt his fate would be one of the topics.

Since he had arrived, no one had tried to harm him, which was encouraging but possibly misleading. For all Flavius knew, the Indians were biding their time, awaiting the tribal council's decision. Should his death be decreed, the same people who had politely accepted the wood and water he brought earlier would just as politely carve out his heart and feed it to the camp dogs. That happened once, to a captive of the Creeks. Or so the story went.

The old crone returned. She got the fire going, set up her pot, and made rabbit stew. The aroma grew thick enough to cut with a tomahawk, so heady and tantalizing that Flavius's mouth would not stop watering. He eyed the bubbling broth as a gold-crazed prospector would eye a rich vein.

A tin pot, he noted, not the type made from a buffalo paunch. A clue that at some time or other, these Indians had had dealings with white men. His fondest wish was that they traded with white traders on a regular basis. If so, somehow he would get word to those traders. Maybe effect a rescue.

It was the sole spark of hope that flickered in Flavius's breast, the spark he refused to let die, the salvation he longed for. It bolstered him when despair tore at his vitals. It kept him together when he felt like falling apart.

The younger woman showed up with a friend, who tried to act indifferent but could not keep her eyes off him. He was used to it. All day Indians had stared at him as he went about the crone's business. Everyone was curious about him, from the youngest sprout to the oldest hag.

Flavius grinned at the young women, and regretted it. The crone tore into him like a riled painter, giving him a licking that he would not soon forget. She was so mad, she didn't feed him. She ladled out stew to the younger ones and a heaping bowl for herself, but not a lick for Flavius.

"It ain't fair," he groused.

The camp quieted. It was the supper hour, the time when families gathered, when the warriors came in from the prairie and the women were done with the day's work and the children were tuckered out from their playful antics. Flavius rested his cheek on a blanket and bemoaned the cruel fate that had delivered him into the clutches of savages.

He still did not know the name of the tribe. Twice he had

tried to find out from the crone, only to receive a whack for his efforts.

One good note. They weren't Apaches. Flavius did not know exactly where Apaches lived, but he did know they inhabited deep caves high in the mountains, that they filed their teeth to points, that they feasted on human flesh, and that they were, on average, seven feet tall. His good friend Melvin Wurst had told him so, and Melvin should know, having read five or six books in his day.

Flavius attempted to remember the names of all the tribes Davy had mentioned, but it was impossible. Davy was a storehouse of information, soaking up tidbits as a sponge soaked up water. Those same danged tidbits kindled Davy's imagination and made him hanker after parts unknown.

"Look at where that got us," Flavius said. The women paid no heed. They were accustomed to his quirky habit of talking to himself, a habit he did not have when he originally left Tennessee.

The old witch rose. Flavius backed against the hide and raised his arms to defend himself. But she brought over a bowl, not her cane. Gruffly, she thrust it into his hands, then shuffled to the fire, muttering.

Flavius did not waste a second. He wolfed the meal so fast, he was licking the bowl clean before he realized he had eaten every last morsel. A huge burp escaped him, and he tensed. Back home, if he so much as uttered a tiny belch, Matilda lit into him with her powder primed. Belching was for pigs, she maintained. And she had not married a pig.

It was one of the few compliments she ever paid him.

Content, Flavius closed his eyes and rubbed his stomach. By his reckoning he was ten to fifteen pounds lighter than he had been when they started. Another couple of months and he would be slimmer than he had been since he crawled out of the cradle.

He was getting ahead of himself. What made him think he would live out the night, let alone another two months?

As if in answer, the flap parted and in marched three burly warriors. Flavius figured they would bind him, but they simply hauled him out and across to the large lodge. The hum of voices fell on his ears as he was shoved inside. Tripping, he had to fling an arm against the side for support. Silence fell, a silence so complete and unnerving that Flavius wanted to bolt.

Two dozen of the most prominent warriors were present. They sat in a semicircle, staring at him. At their head was the same stocky warrior who had greeted the war party upon its return. Flavius smiled wanly and looked around for a place to sit. The question was solved by two of his escorts, who pushed him to a spot in the middle and shoved him to his knees.

"Howdy," Flavius said lamely.

The warriors resumed their deliberations. They were dressed in the Indian equivalent of Sunday-go-to-meeting clothes. Beaded buckskins, clean moccasins, feathers in their hair, the whole works.

"What is your name?"

Several seconds went by before it sank in that Flavius had heard *English*. Blankly, he gaped at the ring of stony faces. "Who—?" he bleated.

"I asked your name, white dog."

The speaker was the chief, the stocky man who packed more solid muscle on his powerful frame than any two warriors. Piercing dark eyes fixed on Flavius, devouring him. They complemented a hawkish nose and peaked lips.

"Harris, sir. Flavius Harris, from Tennessee by way of Kentucky and Maryland. There's been a terrible misunderstanding—"

The leader slashed a finger at the frontiersman. "Quiet, snake. You chatter like a woman. I will ask questions. You will answer them."

Gulping, Flavius nodded. Here was someone it would not do to trifle with. The man's bearing, his tone, his every

110

movement were those of someone who was accustomed to having his way, and woe to anyone stupid enough to buck him.

"You wonder how I speak your tongue? I learned from a trader, from a missionary, from others. I am Two Claws. You have heard of me?"

"No," Flavius confessed. "Can't say as I have. But as I was telling you, I'm not from these parts. If you were a Creek, it's likely I'd know who you are, since the important Creeks are pretty well known in the canebrake—"

The leader held his hand aloft. "You do it again, snake. Once more, and I will have your left thumb cut off. Would you like that?"

Flavius shook his head so vigorously his teeth rattled.

Leaning forward, the man made a tent of his thick fingers. "Let us understand each other, white man. I hate your kind. I hate what your people have done. I hate what they plan to do." Thunder and lightning formed on his beetling brow. "You act confused. Tell me that you are not aware your people have moved onto land which has been ours since the beginning of all things. Tell me that your people do not intend to take *all* our land. That they do not want to drive us to new territory, make us live where we do not want to live."

"I couldn't," Flavius said. "That would be a lie. Our government did the same thing with the Creeks and others."

"You admit it?"

"Why not? I didn't have a hand in it." Not the relocating, anyway. Flavius deemed it best not to mention his participation in the Creek War.

"You are white."

"So? I don't own a parcel of your land. Neither did my pa, or his pa. None of my kin ever did. And as far as I'm concerned, your people can live here until Armageddon."

The leader straightened. "Ar-ma-ged-on," he repeated. "This is a new word. What does it mean?"

"The end times," Flavius said. "When the Devil and the

111

Lord get to slugging it out over who rules Creation.'' That, in a nutshell, was the gist of the many sermons the parson had delivered on the subject.

"I know it not," the man said. "But you are right. This land will be ours long after your kind has come to an end. Comanches are not Pimas or Otoes. We do not break in a strong wind. We bend, then snap back stronger than before."

Finally, Flavius had learned who his captors were. Davy had mentioned something about them once, but for the life of him, Flavius could not recollect what it had been.

The leader grew animated. His hand closed on empty air as if on a throat, and he declared, "We will crush your people. We will drive them from our land. We will send them back to where they came from. Life will be as it was."

The man was deluding himself. Flavius knew that he was not the smartest person alive, but he was smart enough to realize there was no turning back the clock. "I'd be in your debt if you'd see fit to send me back to where I come from. Some food, some water, and I'm out of your hair. What do you say?"

"I say your thumb will hang from my necklace."

"What?"

Two Claws barked commands. The burly trio who had escorted Flavius to the council lodge now surrounded him. His arms were seized. The third man drew a long, shiny blade, then grasped the Tennessean's left wrist.

Flavius was too shocked to move. Shocked, and outright scared. He imagined the blade shearing through his thumb, imagined blood spurting and the agony he must endure. "Please, no," he said, clenching his hand tight. To resist violently might only make the situation worse. Instead of a thumb, Two Claws might elect to punish him by having every finger chopped off. Maybe the whole hand.

The warrior with the knife gripped Flavius's left thumb and attempted to pry it wide. Flavius resisted. In retaliation, one of the other warriors seized him by the hair and brutally snapped his head back. The man prying at his thumb succeeded in raising it an inch. Flavius saw the keen edge of the blade aligned over the bottom joint.

"I don't deserve this!"

A new voice intruded. Someone Flavius could not see was addressing the council in their own tongue. The warrior about to separate his digit from his palm looked up. So did the men holding his arms. Two Claws did not seem any too happy about the interruption and glowered at the party responsible.

Suddenly, to Flavius's immense joy, the warriors let go. The man with the knife stepped back and sheathed the weapon. A strange weakness afflicted Flavius, and everything spun before his eyes. He sank onto all fours.

Two Claws was arguing with someone. Flavius twisted to learn who his benefactor was. The voice was vaguely familiar, as it should be, since it belonged to the tall warrior who had led the war party that captured him. Other leaders joined in, the older ones mainly. The younger men who sat near the entrance did not participate as much.

At length Two Claws turned to Flavius. The crooked smirk was plastered in place. "Your white god protects you. You can keep your thumb, snake."

Flavius yearned to know what the argument had been about, but he was loath to open his mouth.

Two Claws nodded at the tall warrior. "See him? He looks like a man, does he not? He dresses like a man. He sits in the councils of men. But he is a woman. He thinks we should talk peace with your kind. Thinks we can share our land." Two Claws snorted. "Otter Belt is soft. I am not."

Still, Flavius would not risk angering the firebrand by saying anything.

"I want to kill you. Slowly, as is fitting for an enemy. But Otter Belt says we should keep you as a slave. That you do not deserve death. That it was not you who killed my sister's son." Hatred contorted Two Claws's countenance. "Who did it is not important. All whites are the same."

Flavius glanced at Otter Belt, who was huddled with others. Only a couple of warriors were paying attention to Two Claws. Apparently, few Comanches were fluent in English to any degree, which was just his bad luck. It would have been interesting to see how Otter Belt took to being branded a woman.

"You were not alone," Two Claws continued. "We will find your friends. And we will kill the one who shot Yellow Rope." The warrior drummed his fingers on a knee. "As for you, the council must decide."

Flavius was slow-witted at times, but he was not stupid. He knew this meant Two Claws would do his utmost to convince the assembled leaders that they should put him to death, while Otter Belt and a few others would press to have him spared.

Springing to his feet, Flavius faced the men on either side of Otter Belt. As he had done out on the prairie, he made the hand sign for "friend." Shifting a quarter-turn to the right, he repeated the gesture, and again another quarter-turn, until he was facing Otter Belt once more. The tall warrior wore a knowing smile.

Two Claws was not amused. "You think to save yourself? You are mistaken. Whites can never be our friends. The grass will run red with your blood, or it will run red with ours. There is no other way."

Flavius had about had his fill of the warrior's smug arrogance. "As my grandma used to say, a few bad apples don't spoil the whole bunch. Yes, some white men are worthless. So are some Injuns." He stared pointedly at Two Claws. "But a lot of whites are damned decent. My pard, Davy, for instance. A finer person never drew breath. And he thinks like Otter Belt does, that the white man and the red man can live together in peace."

"Another fool. Another dreamer."

"Who are you to judge? I'll bet you've never given it a chance."

"Tell me, fat one. If a man came into your lodge and took your blanket, would you let him keep it? If he came back and demanded food, would you smile and let him have all he wanted? If he shot your dog, would you do nothing? If he pushed you out of your lodge and moved in himself, would you leave?" Two Claws did not wait for a reply. "No, you would not. Neither will we."

Flavius opened his mouth to debate the point but did not. As much as he despised Two Claws, the Comanche was right. Most of the tribes on hand to greet the Pilgrims when they landed at Plymouth Rock, and those who later welcomed the spreading white tide with open arms, had been either erased from the face of the earth or uprooted and pushed steadily westward.

An exchange between Two Claws and the three husky warriors resulted in Flavius's being taken to the crone's lodge. The old woman and the young one were making a parfleche. They barely gave him a glance.

Seated on a blanket, Flavius pondered. His fate now rested in the hands of a couple of dozen men who had every reason to hate him for the color of his skin alone. He was not optimistic.

Someone once mentioned to him that when it came time for a man to meet his Maker, it was best to put one's house in order. Not that Flavius had much to settle. The farm automatically went to Matilda, along with their meager savings. Two hundred and forty dollars. All they had to show for years of scrimping and saving.

As for whether Flavius would be admitted past those pearly gates on high, or whether he was destined for hotter climes, he could not venture a guess. He'd never been the most religious of souls, but neither had he been the most *ir*religious. Like most folks, he'd tended to walk the straight and narrow one misstep at a time.

Funny, isn't it, how a person really doesn't give much thought to the Hereafter until they're poised at the brink? Flavius reflected. People took it for granted from one day to the next that they would be alive to welcome the next dawn. They shouldn't. Death was like a thief in the night, like a shadow constantly at one's shoulder, like a creeping cold frost. It struck without warning, without mercy, without favorites. Rich or poor, kind or cruel, white or red, tall or short, it made no difference.

Flavius was getting a headache. Deep thinking was a habit he had always shied away from.

Someone slapped the flap. The old woman called out, and in walked the three warriors. Without comment they bustled Flavius to the big lodge. Inside, it was quiet as a tomb. Conversation had ceased. The council members sat straight and stiff. Few would meet his gaze.

Flavius shivered, but not from any chill. He was prodded to the center again, with warriors on either side and another behind. In case he bolted, he guessed. Otter Tail nodded at him.

"We have decided," Two Claws announced, getting directly to the point.

His fear grew, but Flavius would not let it show. "How will it be?"

"You will live."

Flavius was unsure whether his ears were working correctly. "I will?" Hope took root, billowing like a sheet in a gale wind.

"If you tell us how many were with you. And where we can find them."

The crashing noise Flavius swore he heard was his death knell. "As to how many there were, that's my business. Where they went after we parted company, I can't say. Likely to St. Louis, where I should be right now. In a tavern, guzzling ale and eating roast pork." He could practically feel

116

the greasy, hot haunch in his hands, could practically taste the salty, fatty meat.

"I do not believe you," Two Claws declared.

"Who are you kidding? You wouldn't believe anything your own mother said if she had a smidgen of white blood in her veins." Flavius squared his shoulders. "Do with me as you will, you heathen bastard."

Two Claws rose onto a knee, his knife partially drawn. "I would cut out your tongue. But I want to hear you scream, hear you beg me to spare you."

The council members rose. Flavius was seized. In a body, the warriors filed outdoors and across the open space to a point midway between the lodges. A post had been erected. Some of the men disappeared, only to show up shortly bearing firewood and buffalo droppings. The material was piled high around the pole—waist high, to be exact.

Word spread. From every lodge they came, somber men, women, and children, to form a gigantic ring.

"I'm to be burned at the stake," Flavius said to himself, unwilling to accept that it was happening. Panic gushed through him and he looked wildly, desperately about, as would any condemned man, for salvation that was not there. He dug in his heels when he was dragged toward the post, but they overpowered him. Slammed against it, he had to submit to having his ankles and wrists bound.

Two Claws, Otter Belt, and other leaders were in front of him. "I would cut you up, piece by piece," said Two Claws. "They want this way."

Flavius saw the crone and the young woman. Was he deluding himself, or did regret etch the old woman's features? He tested the rope, which bit into his skin. It would require the might of a Samson to break free. "Lord Almighty, have mercy," he breathed.

Through the throng hastened a warrior holding a blazing torch. Striding to the pile, he paused and looked at the tribal

117

elders. Wind fanned the flames, their hiss eerily loud.

The pale glow lent the assembled Comanches a ghostly hue. To Flavius they appeared not quite human.

Two Claws motioned, and the warrior lowered the torch.

Chapter Nine

The Texians did not seem to mind the slow progress they were making. At least Farley, Taylor, and Ormbach never complained, but Kerr grumbled constantly. A surly character with little sense of humor, Lucius Kerr was one of those people who thrived on hate. He loathed Indians, and he never let an opportunity to mention how he felt slip by.

"Comanches are the worst of the lot," the grungy Texian was saying as their party moved toward a series of low hills. "They'll slit your throat as soon as look at you. And they're real partial to white women, if'n you take my drift."

"Did they kidnap someone close to you?" Davy Crockett asked. It would explain the man's hatred, if not justify it.

"Naw," Kerr said, and idly scratched his armpit. "I tagged along just for the chance to kill a few of the sons of bitches." Exposing his yellow teeth, he snatched his butcher knife out and slashed it at the air. "I love to chop the vermin into little pieces. Once, down Brazos way, I got to torture a red buck for three days. Put out his eyes, peeled his skin in strips, hacked off his fingers, everything, and not once did that mangy Injun let out a peep. Tough one, he was."

"What had he done to deserve it?"

"Done?" Kerr laughed without mirth. "Hell, mister. He was a Comanche. That was enough." Davy's disgust must have shown, because Kerr glared and added, "I wouldn't expect someone from Tennessee to understand. You don't know how it is in Texas. What we've had to endure."

"Tennessee's had its share of Indian troubles," Davy mentioned. "Ever heard of the Creeks?"

"Can't say as I have, but they don't hold a candle to the Comanches," Kerr avowed. "I'd be willin' to wager that the Comanches slaughter more white folks in one year than your Creeks ever have. They're mean, clever, bloodthirsty. Worthy enemies."

"You almost sound proud of them."

Kerr thought about that a moment. "Maybe I am. As much as I dislike 'em, I have to admit they don't take any guff off anybody. And no one's ever accused them of being puny, like the Pimas and Maricopas and whatnot." He scratched again. "Still, scum is scum. Know what I mean?"

Nodding, Davy goaded the bay he was on forward, to catch up with Farley. He could take only so much of Kerr's company before the man grated on him like sandpaper on metal. The slim arms around his waist moved, and Becky's head poked past his left elbow.

"Mr. Kerr is a lot like my grandfather was," she whispered.

For one so young, she's very smart, Davy mused. Both men shared certain qualities: They were vicious, self-centered, and so full of spite it seeped out their ears. He patted her arm. "Don't let him spook you. Men like Kerr are so soured on life, they never get the acid out of their systems."

Davy and the girl were not the only ones riding double. Heather was with Farley, Taylor with Ormbach. They switched a lot, as the whim struck them. Kerr usually rode alone; no one particularly cared to ride double with him.

Heather heard them and shifted. "How are you holding up, sweetheart?" she asked her daughter.

"I'm fine," Becky said, in that tone children use when their parents treat them like children. "I'm just like I was before we left St. Louis."

They were all fully recovered, thanks to the Texians. The four never went thirsty. They knew where every stream, spring, and river was located. Taylor, especially, was as familiar with the land and the wildlife as Davy was with the back of his own hand. Years back, Taylor had been a buffalo hunter and got to know the country well.

Ormbach was a farmer, plain and simple. As strong as an ox, he was not the most quick-witted of the group, but he was as dependable as the day was long. He did not share Kerr's fanatical hatred. Ormbach was along because his good friend Taylor had come.

As for Farley, he had obtained a land grant from the Mexican government and was looking to establish a thriving ranch. From what Davy could gather from hints dropped by the others, Farley had a reputation for being honest and true, and incredibly fast with those fancy pistols of his. He also had a reputation for being highly popular with the ladies of San Antonio, so much so, he was considered a bit of a rake.

Heather Dugan had certainly fallen under his spell. Or maybe it was the other way around. They spent most of their time together. Heather preferred to ride with him over anyone else. At night they sat together, whispering and laughing and brushing against each other like a couple of lovestruck youngsters.

Davy was glad for Heather. After the hell she had been through, she deserved some happiness. Taylor and Ormbach made no comments about the situation, but they grinned a lot behind Farley's back. It did not seem to sit well with Kerr, though. On several occasions Davy caught him glaring at the couple when they were not aware. What it portended, Davy could not guess.

Now Farley pointed at the hills and said, "Once we reach those, we have to keep our eyes skinned. Two Claws favors this region at this time of year. Word has it that last summer he camped on the other side for three or four months." Sadness clouded his handsome face. "I just pray Marcy and Beth are still with them."

Marcy was Farley's sister, Beth his cousin. As Davy understood the story, Marcy had been visiting Beth when the Comanches struck. The farm owned by Beth's father was one of the farthest from the settlements, so even though neighbors heard shots and screams and rushed to help, it was all over by the time aid got there. Beth's father had been severely wounded, left a cripple, his wife and oldest son slain. Marcy and Beth had been taken captive. The strain proved too much for Farley's father, whose heart later gave out. Farley's mother was anxiously waiting in town for word of the rescue attempt.

"And I pray they'll go back with us."

Heather straightened. "What an odd remark. Why in the world wouldn't they?"

"It's been a year," Farley said.

"How old was your sister when she was taken?" Davy asked.

"Sixteen. Childbearing age."

Davy dropped the subject. He knew what the Texian was hinting at, but evidently Heather did not.

"Are you saying that if she's had a baby, she'll want to stay with the Comanches?"

"It happens all the time," Farley said. "So far those red devils have stolen over fifty women, and only two have ever been recovered. Most would rather stay with their children than come back to the life they knew."

"Even if they can bring the children with them?"

Farley grew sadder. "That's just it. They can't. The Comanches aren't idiots. Whenever a parley is set up to swap for a captive, they won't let the mothers take the kids.''

"Well, then, *steal* the mothers and the kids.''

"Which is exactly what we aim to do,'' Farley declared. "No parley. No truce. No trade. We go in, we get them, we bring them out. And we kill anyone who stands in our way.''

Four against an entire village? Davy did not think much of the odds, although he admired the Texians' pluck. Unfortunately, it put the Dugans in great danger. "Why not send Taylor or Ormbach back with Heather and Becky?'' he suggested.

"What?'' the blonde said.

Farley nodded. "I've been thinking of doing just that. We'll talk it over once we make camp. The last thing I want is for anything to happen to them.''

"Hold on,'' Heather protested. "I should have some say in the matter. And I'm not going anywhere.''

"Think of your daughter,'' Farley said.

"I am. We'd be at just as much risk. This is Comanche territory, and they can show up anywhere at any time. I'm staying with you, come what may.''

Becky squeezed Davy and stated, "The same with me. Mr. Crockett hasn't let us come to any harm yet.''

Davy caught Farley's eye, and they both frowned. Heather was making a mistake that might cost her life and that of her child. But short of trussing her up and throwing her over a horse, what could they do?

The hills were barren, rent by ravines and gulches. A tiny spring provided water. As they unsaddled and set up camp beside it, Taylor mentioned, "We're fairly safe here. The Comanches won't set foot within half a mile. To them, these hills are bad medicine. Something to do with a chief who died under mysterious circumstances ages ago.''

"Mysterious?'' Davy said.

Taylor tugged his saddle off. "A 'breed told me the tale. It seems that a band was out hunting buffalo and stopped for the night at this spring. Around midnight, the chief got up and walked off. To relieve himself, probably. Anyway, he had been gone only a few seconds when the others heard him cry out, something like, 'Who's there?' Then they heard him scream, the most god-awful scream anyone ever heard. It scared them stiff, and Comanches don't scare easily. They grabbed their weapons and ran to find out what had happened." Pausing, Taylor glanced at Becky.

"You can tell us," she said sweetly. "I don't believe in ghosts anymore."

"This was no ghost, missy," Taylor said. "They found that chief torn apart. Arms, legs, even his head was separated from his body. And they found huge bloody prints, tracks three times the size of a man's."

Heather had become interested. "Was it a grizzly or a cat?"

"Neither. Whatever it was, it walked on two legs. And each foot had only three toes."

"That's impossible."

Taylor shrugged. "You'd think so, wouldn't you? But the old-timers and the Indians claim that they've seen apes in these parts. Hairy, smelly varmints. Three-toed skunk apes, some call them."

"I've never heard anything so ridiculous in my life," Heather said.

Davy was reminded of stories he'd heard while on the campaign against the Creeks. Down in Florida—so the accounts went—deep, deep in the swamps, lived savage red apes that would tear a man limb from limb without provocation. One scout swore on the Bible that a trapper he'd known had gone off into the swampland and never emerged. Friends canoed in to look for him and located his camp, plus what little was left of the man, mainly tattered clothes and gnawed bones. They also found tufts of red hair. Davy had dismissed the account as another liquor-induced tall tale. Maybe he was wrong.

Becky surveyed the shadowed nook in which they were going to bed down. "Have any of you seen one of these apes?"

"No," Taylor said. "They're mighty rare, if they're around at all."

Kerr grunted. "Who cares if they are? A shot between the eyes will fetch 'em to eternity just like it will everything else." He swelled his chest and hefted his rifle. "I ain't afeared of any critter, two-legged or otherwise."

Taylor had taken a spyglass from his saddlebags. "Crockett, I'd like some company," he announced. "We'll have us a look-see at what's on the other side of these hills."

A game trail wound up to the summit of the last one. Calling it a summit was a stretch; the crown reared a lofty thirty feet above the plain. But even from that low height they were granted a magnificent vista. Mile after mile of gently waving grass broken by knolls and hillocks spread to the far horizon.

Perhaps two miles off lay a waterway rimmed by vegetation. Cottonwoods dotted its course.

Taylor opened the spyglass and pressed it to his right eye. "One of the reasons I brought you up here," he said as he swung the glass back and forth, "was to warn you about Kerr. If any warning is needed." He pursed his lips. "You impress me as being highly intelligent. Need I go on?"

"A few particulars would be nice. I'm not nearly as smart as I pretend to be."

The Texian chuckled. "Very well." He roved the glass along the stream. "Kerr is not to be trusted. He has a nasty temper, and he likes to have his own way."

"Beating around the bush, are we?" Davy hunkered, propping Liz between his legs. "As my grandma used to say, you don't collect many eggs walking around the chicken coop. You have to go inside."

Lowering the spyglass, Taylor looked down. "Very well. It's Miss Dugan I'm worried about. Haven't you noticed how

125

Kerr has been brazenly admiring her? How he ogles her at night when she's asleep?''

"If he lays a hand on her, Farley will shoot him," Davy predicted.

"Probably. But I wouldn't put it past Kerr to bury a blade in Farley's back, then make his move." Taylor squatted. "I was against bringing that ruffian along, but other than Orm-bach, no one else would join us. It's suicide, they said."

"They have their own families to think of."

"You're being charitable. Frankly, they wanted no part of our mad scheme. Stalking Comanches in Comanche territory is not for the timid. And planning to sneak into a village and spirit captives from under their very noses is as insane as butting heads with a bull buffalo."

"So you brought Kerr along because you needed an extra gun," Davy said. "No use crying over spilt milk. It was the right thing to do." He held out his hand, and Taylor gave him the telescope. "As for Heather, don't fret. She can take care of herself. She has one of my pistols, and she's not afraid to use it."

"Are you always so agreeable?"

"Not according to my wife." Through the spyglass the distant trees were magnified ten times. Davy had the illusion he could reach out and touch them. He studied the growth lining the bank, raised the glass a few inches, and saw conical shapes materialize in the haze. "Take a gander," he said. "Just south of those forked cottonwoods."

The Texian complied. "Dog my cats! You found the village! It can't be more than three miles, as the crow flies."

Movement to the west alerted Davy to a group of riders. Grabbing Taylor, he flattened. Nine warriors, he counted, heading home after a hunt or a raid. Had they seen a glint of light on the hilltop? One of them seemed to be pointing at the hills. He watched with bated breath until the group forded the stream and was hidden by the trees. "We'd better lay low until dark."

"My sentiments exactly."

A small fire blazed next to the spring. Heather was adding dry twigs and had a pile at her feet. Davy ran over, scattered the pile with a kick, and hurriedly scooped water onto the flames, putting out every last one. He swatted at stray tendrils of smoke with his coonskin cap, dispelling them.

Initially startled, Heather demanded, "What did you do that for?"

Taylor told them about the village.

Farley flushed with excitement and wagged his fists. "At last! We've done it! By this time tomorrow, Marcy and Beth could be on their way to San Antonio."

"What's your plan?" Davy asked.

Farley arched an eyebrow. "Plan? We don't rightly have one. I reckon we'll sneak on down, figure out which lodges the women are in, and take them by force."

Davy snapped his fingers. "Just like that?"

"I know. I know," Farley said. "I'm open to any ideas." He pointed at Davy, Taylor, and Ormbach. "Be ready to go an hour after sunset. Kerr will stay to guard Heather and Becky and the horses."

Kerr? Davy noticed that he was not the only one uncomfortable with the notion. Taylor fidgeted, Ormbach frowned. The heady thrill of saving Marcy had muddied Farley's thinking. "I hear that Kerr is a good shot," Davy said tactfully, even though no one had made any such claim. "Maybe we should take him and leave Ormbach."

"Whatever you want," Farley said absently.

Kerr cleared his throat. "I'm staying. I agreed to help find the village, not go into it." He offered an olive branch. "Don't worry. I'll cover you if the Comanches are dogging your heels."

Davy was in a quandary. He'd as soon leave Heather with a rabid wolf as with Kerr. He would stay himself, but while the others rescued the women he was going after Flavius. The only other solution he could see was to propose,

127

"Maybe we should all go. Stick together for safety's sake."

"You're being silly," Heather said. "Becky and I will be fine. Do what you have to."

That ended that. Farley unpacked a dress he had brought for his sister and smoothed it on a flat rock. "Yellow," he said as Davy strolled by. "It was always her favorite color. I figured this would cheer her some."

Davy brought up a question that had been eating at him since their talk that morning. "What if she refuses to go with us, no matter what?"

"I'll cross that bridge when I get to it," Farley reponded. Gently, he ran a finger over the soft fabric. "But she won't. We were always close, Marcella and me. As kids, we always played together. Tag. Hide-and-seek. You name it. She was fun to be with." A haunted aspect tainted his expression, and his voice dropped to a whisper. "I can't begin to imagine how she's suffered. Well, no more. I aim to end it, one way or another."

Davy did not like the sound of that. "If she won't come, there isn't much you can do."

"You're wrong, friend. There's always a last resort." Farley unconsciously drifted a hand to one of his ivory-handled flintlocks. "My mother made it clear. Under no circumstances is Marcy to stay with the Comanches."

Horrified, Davy moved closer so none of the others would overhear. "Your own mother wants you to shoot your sister? How can she?"

Farley's eyes were focused inward. "What do you do if your horse breaks a leg? You kill it to put it out of its misery. This is no different."

"The hell it isn't. People aren't animals. And it's your *sister*, for God's sake."

"All the more reason I can't let her go on suffering. Just to think of her being abed with a Comanche—" Farley broke off and shuddered. "The shame is more than anyone should have to bear."

Shame for whom? Davy was inclined to ask, but he held his tongue. It was a family affair, to be settled between mother, son, and daughter. "What about your cousin Beth? Are you supposed to kill her, too?"

"Her pa left that up to me."

The young man was shouldering an inhuman burden. "I wouldn't want to be in your shoes," Davy remarked, and walked to where Heather and Becky were munching on jerked buffalo meat, courtesy of Taylor. "We need to have a few words," he bluntly told the mother.

Heather checked to make sure no one else was within earshot. "Is it about Kerr? If so, save your breath."

"How did you guess?"

"Taylor and Ormbach beat you to the punch. They both warned me not to let down my guard while the rest of you are gone." She rested her fingers on the flintlock the Tennessean had lent her. "I'll tell you the same thing I told them. Don't fuss over us. If Kerr so much as looks at me crosswise, I'll part his hair with lead."

"Aim about three feet lower," Davy advised, winking.

Night came on apace. Coyotes were serenading the stars when Taylor called the others together. "It's time," he said. Guns were checked once more. Knives were loosened in their sheaths. Davy had honed his tomahawk while waiting; now he rubbed a hand over the cold steel, glad he had it for close-quarter combat.

Kerr had been oddly quiet the whole evening. Davy rated it a bad sign, but there was nothing he could do. They were committed. Besides, Heather had closed her ears to their earnest appeals for her to go along. Like most females, she had an independent streak a mile wide, and woe to any man who treated her as if she could not take care of herself.

Davy was the last to leave. At a bend in the trail, he glanced over a shoulder. Heather was seated on a rock, Becky fiddling with a folding knife Taylor had given her. Dark shadows partially hid Kerr. "Take care," he called quietly. Mother and daughter waved. Kerr did not move.

Once past the hills, the Texians advanced in single file, Farley in the lead. Through low grass they stealthily slunk to the stream. There, Taylor shimmied up a cottonwood. The village was peaceful, he reported. East of it milled an enormous horse herd.

A quarter-moon afforded enough light to see by but not enough to give them away from a distance. Farley paralleled the stream until he discovered a gravel bar that enabled them to ford without getting wet above the knees. They had a scary few moments when something snorted and bounded off through the brush. It was only a deer.

The barking of a dog heightened their caution. Every Comanche, Taylor had informed Davy, owned at least one, and were quite attached to them. Unlike some tribes, who routinely ate dog flesh, Comanches would no more devour one than they would a friend or family member.

Farley's eagerness nearly did them in. They were five hundred yards from the lodges when he stepped on a twig that crunched loudly. All four of them instantly froze. Davy listened but heard only the breeze. He waited for the Texians to continue and was puzzled when they didn't. Rustling to the left explained why.

A Comanche boy of twelve or so was heading toward the village. Over his shoulder was slung a bow and quiver; in his left hand was a rabbit. He had heard the twig, and stopped.

Davy saw Taylor start to draw his knife. Slaying children did not sit well with him, and he was debating whether to rush the boy before Taylor could when the young Comanche ambled on. The boy could not be blamed for being so careless. No one in recent memory had attacked a Comanche village. They were the lords of their domain, undisputed masters of the southern prairie, able to hold their own against even the dreaded Apaches.

When the boy was gone, Farley cat-footed forward. The

magnitude of the challenge they faced became apparent when they were on their bellies in tall grass at the camp's edge. Davy had never beheld so many lodges in one place. Locating Flavius and the missing women would be next to impossible.

A number of lodge flaps were wide open. Fires lit the interiors, showing tranquil scenes of families enjoying their evening meals.

Davy had not thought to ask how Farley would identify the captives. Whites kept among Indians any length of time tended to become like their captors. Their skin was burnt brown. They wore buckskins, let their hair grow. Telling the white women apart from Comanche women might be difficult.

As for Flavius, he would stick out like a ram in a wolf pack. A crude comparison, but apt. The Tennessean examined the entrance to every dwelling.

Suddenly warriors began to file from a large lodge. Davy was elated to recognize Flavius among them. His pulse quickened as his friend was led to a post and tied fast. Kindling was brought, enough to burn a grown man to a crisp, while more and more Comanches gathered. Flavius looked on, helpless.

Farley crawled to Davy's side. "Is that your partner?" he whispered.

"Afraid so."

"That smirking bastard in front of him is Two Claws."

Davy was more interested in a warrior who emerged from a lodge bearing a burning brand. The man hurried toward the post, toward the waiting wood that would incinerate Flavius. In another minute the conflagration would be lit.

Do something! Davy's mind screamed.

But what?

Chapter Ten

Flavius Harris braced to meet his doom. The heat from the torch singed his buckskins as the warrior slowly lowered it to the wood. Two Claws looked on, smirking smugly. The torch was inches from the pile when a woman in the crowd yelled shrilly and pointed. All the Comanches glanced up. The man with the torch hesitated, as dumbfounded as the rest.

Davy Crockett was the cause. Ninety seconds earlier he had leaped to his feet and dashed toward the nearest lodge. Farley snatched at his leg, whispering, "What in the devil do you think you're doing?" But Davy did not answer. Every second was crucial.

The flap to the lodge was open. Inside, in the center, burned a cooking fire. Davy raced to it, gripped the end of a long burning brand, and ran back out again. Applying the brand to the edge of the flap, he set it ablaze. The instant it ignited, he whirled and ran to its neighbor to do the same.

Then he dashed into the night. At the grass he stopped and flung the brand at a third lodge.

Davy ducked down just as a woman cried out. The first lodge had flames half a foot high licking at the hide, the second lodge was beginning to burn, and the third had not yet ignited. It was enough to bring the Comanches on the run. Shouting in a confused chorus, the villagers rushed toward the afflicted dwellings.

Davy rolled to the left—not a few yards but more than a score. Shoving into a crouch, he sped around the perimeter of the encampment until he was abreast of the post. All the Indians save one were now at the lodges. The sole exception was the warrior who had been about to set Flavius on fire. The man still held the torch.

Without hesitation Davy veered toward the middle of the encampment, running flat out. All it would take was for a single Comanche to spot him and the whole band would be out for his blood. But he did not care. He had to save Flavius. It helped that the Comanches had their backs to him, and that the warrior by the post had riveted his attention to the attempts to save the tepees.

Flavius struggled against his bounds. He had loosened his left wrist at the cost of considerable skin, and could feel blood trickling down his arm. The patter of running feet made him twist. Never in his entire life had any sight been as welcome as that of the brawny Irishman rushing out of the darkness with Liz raised on high.

The warrior heard Davy at the last second. Pivoting, the man thrust the torch at him and opened his mouth to call out. Another bound brought Davy to his quarry. Sidestepping the sizzling flames, he brought Liz's heavy stock crashing down onto the warrior's brow. The man crumpled like a piece of paper, but as he fell, so did the torch. It landed on the pile.

"Cutting it close, aren't you?" Flavius bantered as the dry tinder flared red and orange.

Davy whipped out his tomahawk. Moving behind the post, he chopped at the ropes. He freed Flavius's wrists but missed with his first swing at the rope lower down. Crackling flames spurted toward his friend's legs.

"Hurry!" Flavius urged.

Davy swung again. The hemp parted. Without delay he rotated and raced into the darkness. They were still in grave peril. As soon as the lodges were safe, the Comanches would realize what had happened. Dozens of maddened warriors would fan out, searching. He bore to the right to circle the village, replacing his tomahawk on the fly.

Flavius wanted to thank his friend for saving his life, but he needed all his breath to keep up. Only one of the lodges still burned, the Comanches buzzing around it like enraged bees. He glimpsed two figures in buckskin dresses apart from the rest, rather meekly standing by themselves in the shadows of a lodge on the perimeter. He feared they would spot Davy and him, but they only had eyes for the fire.

To Flavius's astonishment, Davy unexpectedly angled toward the pair. "Consarn it," Flavius hissed. "What are you doing?"

The taller woman had sandy hair. Davy slowed, approaching them silently. He was taking an awful risk. They might not be the ones the Texians sought. But he owed it to Farley and the others to find out. From ten feet away he put a hand to his mouth and whispered, "Marcella Tanner! Bethany Cole! Is that you?"

The women spun. One, the shorter, held an infant bundled in a blanket.

"Marcy? Beth?" Davy repeated, stepping forward so they could see him. "I'm a friend. I've come to save you. Let's go!" He motioned for them to make haste and turned to leave. But neither woman moved. The short one appeared terrified; the taller woman had a hand to her throat.

"Please," Davy pleaded. "If you're who I think you are,

135

if you want to see your loved ones again, we best light a shuck while we can!''

The woman with the baby had been transformed into granite. The sandy-haired one, though, took a tentative step and said timidly, ''You're white!''

''I'm a friend,'' Davy assured her. The Comanches, he saw, had surrounded the burning lodge, and warriors were flapping at the flames with robes and blankets and whatever else was handy. A sudden burst of light halfway across the village apprised him of the fact that the woodpile and the post were fully aflame. As yet, the Comanches were not aware of it, but they would be at any moment.

''Please,'' Davy repeated, and beckoned.

The tall woman started forward, then stopped cold, staring past Davy. He looked. It was only Flavius. ''Stay where you are,'' he cautioned his friend. ''We don't want to frighten them.''

''Who are they?'' Flavius was sorely confused. His every instinct was to run like hell. To linger was madness.

Davy held his hand out to the sandy-haired woman. ''Are you Marcy?'' When she bobbed her chin, he said, ''Your brother is close by. Would you like to see him? I can take you this very minute.''

''Farley?''

A shriek rang out. A woman over by the burning lodge was to blame. One of the warriors had ventured too close and his shirt had burst into flame. Others converged, swatting at his arm and chest.

Marcy glanced at the Comanches, then at Davy. She took another step, but hesitated.

''What are you waiting for?'' Davy coaxed. ''We have to leave before it's too late.''

It already was.

Around a lodge to the right appeared a dog, a bristly mongrel that bared its fangs and barked ferociously. Davy leveled his rifle, not wanting to shoot but expecting the beast to attack. Simultaneously, screeches rent the air. From out of the inferno devouring the post and the wood darted a human form covered in writhing flames.

Davy was aghast. It was the warrior he had knocked out. The man was a sheet of fire from head to toe. He saw the warrior fall, saw him flop and roll in a frenzy.

Tremendous howls mingled in a chorus of fury. The rest of the Comanches had seen the stricken man, and many were hurrying to his assistance.

"We best go!" Davy pleaded.

Marcy took another step, but Beth backed off, shaking her head and babbling in the Comanche tongue.

To Flavius, that was the last straw. Afraid the women were going to get them killed, he leaped past Davy to the side of the one with the baby, and clutched her arm. "Quit stalling, damn it," he scolded. Up close, he could see that she was white. "What the devil is the matter with you?"

Bethany Cole threw back her head and screamed.

All hell broke loose. Over by the burning lodge and over by the burning post, Comanches heard, and turned. From out of nowhere charged three warriors, the foremost with a war club upraised. Venting war whoops, they bore down on the Tennesseans. Davy snapped off a shot that smashed into the lead warrior's chest and felled him like a poled ox. Davy clawed at his pistol, but the other two warriors were too close. They would be on him before he could shoot.

A human panther sprang onto the scene. Farley Tanner drew his ivory-handled flintlocks in a blur. The twin pistols flashed up and out and boomed in unison. Both Comanches were cored in midstride.

Beth spun and bolted, blubbering in Comanche. But Marcy threw herself at her brother and wrapped her arms around his chest. "Farley! It's you! Really you! After all this time! I'd given up hope!"

"Sis!" the Texian cried, embracing her.

The siblings were so choked by emotion that they were

blind to the onrushing horde. Davy prodded Farley with his rifle and hollered, "Save the reunion for later! Have you forgot where you are?"

Farley tore his gaze from his sister. He glanced at the Comanches, then at the fleeing shape of Bethany Cole. What was going through his mind was not hard to figure out.

"Leave her," Davy said. "If you don't, you'll die."

"But I promised her pa!"

Flavius was backpedaling into the grass. They were insane, the whole lot of them, including Crockett. In another thirty seconds the Comanches would swarm over them like riled bees. They wouldn't stand a prayer. *"Move, damn you!"* he bawled stridently, and suited action to words by rotating on a heel and fleeing. He was shocked nearly witless when two shadows heaved erect in front of him. Fearing they were Comanches, he drew back a fist.

"Hold on! We're on your side, hoss," said an older man.

The other one snapped a rifle to his shoulder and fired. Sixty yards off, a whooping warrior pitched to the ground.

Davy did not wait for Farley to reach a decision. He took a step and shoved brother and sister toward the open prairie. Marcy stumbled, but Farley caught her. Hand in hand, they hastened after Flavius and the others. Davy brought up the rear, unlimbering his pistol. Like a deranged mob of banshees, the Comanches flooded out of the village in fierce pursuit. Six or seven of the fleetest warriors were in the lead, moving so swiftly that the outcome was inevitable.

The Texians were moving as fast as they could, but it was not good enough. Davy slowed a bit, calculating. A desperate gambit might save them, but his own life would hang in the balance. Abruptly whirling, he pointed his flintlock at the first Comanche. Immediately, the man dived flat. Davy swept the gun in an arc and the half-dozen Comanches behind the first imitated their comrade's example.

A few seconds was all it bought. But it permitted Flavius and the Texians to vanish to the north. Davy waited for one

of the Comanches to rise, then pivoted and ran to the northwest, deliberately luring the warriors off. Yipping and yowl-
ing, they took the bait and came after him.

Davy bounded flat out, a jackrabbit chased by a pack of
coyotes. The lead warriors were glued to him, and the main
body of Comanches followed the leaders. He had saved his
friends, but at what cost? Because for the life of him, he did
not know how he was going to shake the pack.

To the north, Flavius Harris was demonstrating that his
bulk was not all excess weight. He kept pace with the strangers, wondering who they were and how they had happened
to hook up with Davy. He could think of fifty questions to
ask, questions that had to wait until he and the strangers were
safe.

He ran beside a big man, the slowest of the bunch. They
were hundreds of yards from the village when he thought to
check on Davy. To his amazement, the Irishman was nowhere to be seen. Nor were the Comanches. "What the
hell!" he exclaimed, slowing. "Where's my pard?"

"He ran a different direction," huffed the big man.

"What?" Flavius nearly stopped, but the man wrapped a
hand the size of a ham around his arm.

"I think he did it on purpose, to shake them off our
scent." The man had a thick drawl, like the other two.
"We'd best keep a-going. Your pard is a canny one. I reckon
he knows what he's doing."

Reluctantly, Flavius allowed himself to be pulled along.
"I don't like this," he muttered. His place was at Davy's
side.

"We'll go back for him if he doesn't show," vowed the
other, and cracked a lopsided smile. "Ben Ormbach, by the
way. I know who you are, Mr. Harris. Davy told us. Me and
my friends are Texians." He said that last proudly, making
it sound as if being from Texas was the highest honor a man
could have.

They ran and ran, cooled by a northerly wind that fanned their perspiring faces. A belt of vegetation marked the location of a stream.

Flavius grew more worried by the minute about Davy. He waded into the water, shivering as a cold sensation spread across his feet and up his legs. On the opposite bank he halted to scour the ground they had covered.

"Kick up your heels, friend," prompted Ormbach.

Flavius came close to plunging back into the water. Hoping that he wasn't making a mistake he would regret forever after, he jogged deeper into the night. The Texians seemed to have a definite destination in mind. Presently, inky mounds reared skyward ahead. Flavius and the Texians threaded in among hills, climbing to the crest of the first.

"We've done it!" Farley declared. Hugging Marcy, he groaned and buried his face in her hair. "I can't believe I'm holding you. I can't believe you're alive and well."

For her part, the woman broke into racking sobs she muffled against his chest. "Oh, Farley. Oh, Farley," she said over and over. "I've prayed and prayed, but I never expected my prayers to be answered."

"Would someone mind telling me what this is all about?" Flavius requested

"Glad to oblige," said the older man, offering a hand. "My handle is Taylor."

Before they moved on, Flavius learned all he needed to. It warmed his heart to hear that Heather and Becky were alive. But it stunned him beyond measure once he fully realized how far south they had traveled, how far from the Mississippi River they had strayed. Would he ever set foot in Tennessee again? Or was he fated to aimlessly wander the earth, a victim of fickle happenstance?

The Texians stepped lively along a narrow trail. They were drunk with victory, Farley and his sister strolling arm in arm. Marcy repeatedly pinched him, as if to prove to herself that he wasn't a figment of her imagination.

Ormbach was whistling softly as they descended to a flat space that bordered a spring. Flavius was as dry as sand inside. He brushed past the big Texian to get a drink, stopping when he saw Ormbach and the others turn every which way, acting confused. "What is it?" he inquired. "What's wrong?"

"They're gone," Taylor bleated.

"Who?"

"Your friends. Kerr. The horses. Everything." Taylor gestured. "This is where we left them."

It was Flavius's turn to groan. Just when he thought the worst was over, he was plunged anew into the unending nightmare.

Taylor voiced similar sentiments. "There's no way we can escape the Comanches now. Come daylight, they'll track us down and wipe us out."

Flavius gazed over the hills at the benighted plain. If only Davy were there! Crockett had a flair for getting out of tight scrapes. But Flavius had to be honest with himself. Maybe, just maybe, their string of luck had played itself out.

Davy Crockett had held to a steady pace for more than five minutes, maintaining a fifteen-yard lead over the swiftest of the Comanches. But he was tiring. And he suspected that the warriors had been waiting for just this moment, that they had held back so they could overpower him easily once he flagged.

What they would do to him was best not thought about. Lodges had been damaged, a warrior burned, others shot. For that he must suffer, suffer as few human beings ever had.

Davy scoured the grassland for the umpteenth time. Somewhere in that general area were stands of cottonwoods. He could lose himself among them if only he could *find* them. He angled to the north, to the south. Nothing. He leaped high into the air. No sign of them.

Gritting his teeth, Davy willed his tired legs to pump for

all they were worth. He tapped into his reserve stamina, pouring all he had into a last effort to elude the human bloodhounds who dogged his steps. His sole consolation, should they overtake him, was that the others had gotten away. Flavius and the Texians would escort Heather and Becky to safety. His sacrifice would not be in vain.

Suddenly a murky tangle of vegetation hove into sight. Davy flew toward it. As the growth assumed definite shape, he spied a dense tangle of undergrowth and barreled on in. A shrill howl greeted his ploy. He heard one of the Comanches crash into the growth in his wake. Veering to the right, Davy fell prone and lay perfectly still except for the hammering of his heart.

Within seconds a burly silhouette barged past. Other Comanches called out and were answered by warriors circling to ensnare him. They assumed that he had gone on through. Splashing noises pegged the whereabouts of the stream.

Davy carefully shifted. Warriors were everywhere now, spreading out, poking into every nook and cranny. Some thrust lances into bushes. Other hacked at dark areas with long knives. He saw women among them, every bit as determined as the men to bring him to bay.

Someone snapped instructions. Peeking over a low thin branch, Davy spotted Two Claws. The leader was a study in frustration. When a warrior came up and said something that Two Claws did not like, the chief pushed him, earning bitter looks from many others.

Placing his chin on a wrist, Davy elected to wait the Comanches out. Eventually they would drift elsewhere and he could bend his steps northward.

The crunch of a twig sent a tingle down his spine. A warrior was six feet to the left, walking directly toward him. Davy put his thumb on the hammer of the pistol. The man covered another two feet. One more stride and Davy would be found.

Two Claws shouted. The nearest warrior and several others stopped what they were doing and hurried to him. Two Claws led them away at a brisk trot.

The night grew still. Comanches were well to the north, to the south, and to the west. Davy was content to stay where he was for the time being. He assumed it was a good sign that there had been no shots since Farley dropped those two warriors. Evidently the Texians and Flavius had escaped and would be waiting for him at the spring.

Gradually the sounds of the hunt faded. Davy let another ten minutes go by for good measure, then slowly rose. Wedging the pistol under his belt, he reloaded Liz, relying on his sense of touch to gauge exactly how much powder to use.

The ramrod scraped against its housing when he yanked it out. Freezing, he listened for an outcry, but there was none. As quietly as he could, he tamped the ball and patch down onto the powder.

Slipping from the thicket, Davy hiked northward. He bent at the waist, sinking lower whenever faint sounds reached him. The Comanches were concentrating their search on the far side of the stream, which meandered northward before curving due east to the south of the hills. Every so often a roving figure was briefly visible.

A feral growl heralded a new threat. Dogs had been brought in.

Davy glanced back. Was his mind playing tricks on him, or were several shadows moving at the limits of his vision? Discarding caution, he ran, and promptly heard a warrior to his rear holler. Answers came from the west and the north.

None, though, from the east. To the east, a mile or so, lay the village. Not all the Comanches had given chase, and they were bound to spot him if he attempted to slip by. They would never expect him to go in that direction. So he did.

The snarl of a dog inspired Davy to pour on the speed, but the animal gained rapidly. He heard the rustle of its body through the high grass, heard the pad of its feet and its wolfish pants. Rather than resort to the rifle and let every Comanche within a thousand yards know where he was, Davy gripped his tomahawk. When the panting was at his heels, he stopped and spun.

The dog was a big shaggy brute. Teeth glinting in the pale starlight, it had already launched itself. Davy swung, the tomahawk slicing into the animal's thick shoulder. He tried to skip aside, but the dog slammed into him and they both toppled. Davy tore the tomahawk out of the animal's hide.

The frontiersman let go of his rifle as he landed and heaved upward. The dog had recovered much more quickly. Crouched low, the beast snarled and pounced, rearing on its hind legs. Claws ripped into Davy's forearm, dug furrows over his ribs. He sank the tomahawk into its side, but the creature was not fazed. It snapped at his wrist, narrowly missing.

Off in the dark a warrior shouted.

Dropping onto all fours, the dog feinted to the right and streaked in on the left, its jaws wide to clamp onto Davy's ankle. Only a frantic leap saved him.

Another shout from the warrior caused the dog to stop and lift its head. Maybe to bark. Davy was off balance, but with a desperate wrench he arced his tomahawk down and in. The razor-sharp edge sliced into the animal's throat.

Davy stood over the twitching animal, breathing heavily. Retrieving Liz, he wiped the tomahawk on his leggings as he ran southward. He had gone more than a hundred yards when an anguished cry let him know the dog had been found.

Would they guess where he was headed? Davy adopted a steady rhythm, pacing himself, conserving his energy.

The village was abuzz with activity, Comanches flitting from spot to spot. Most were women and children, but enough warriors were on hand to pose a problem. Plenty of dogs were conspicuous, most near the burnt lodge.

Well shy of the site, Davy bore to the south. The wind was at his back now, and it brought with it the thud of swift footsteps. Swiveling, he dropped onto a knee. A stocky avenger was after him. He suspected it was the owner of the dog. Either the man had deduced which way he had gone, or the warrior was endowed with exceptional eyesight and could track at night. In confirmation of the latter notion, the Comanche had his head bent to the ground, as if he could see where the stems had been bent.

It would have been child's play to shoot the man dead, or to bury the tomahawk in his torso. But Davy did not want to kill unless he was given no choice. Girding himself, he held Liz firmly, and when the warrior was almost upon him, he thrust himself upward, driving the stock at the man's head.

The Comanche was as quick on his feet as his dog had been. Evading the blow, he produced a knife and speared the tip at the Tennessean's heart.

Davy blocked the blade with Liz. Steel scraped on steel. Reversing himself, he rammed the stock into the warrior's gut. The Comanche doubled over, sputtering, and a swipe of Liz's barrel to his temple took the fight out of him.

To the west voices were raised. Davy adjusted his coonskin cap and jogged on around the village, bearing to the east. He had a plan. As he skirted the last of the lodges, piercing wails fluttered on the breeze. A woman was hunched over the body of the warrior who had been set ablaze.

Davy slowed and scanned the waving grass. At first he mistook the dark mass he sought for part of the plain. It was the unmistakable odor that gave them away. That, and the nickers and whinnies he presently heard. He had found the horse herd.

There were so many he could not decide which one suited him. A mare seemed promising. She stood her ground when he approached, displaying no fear. "Ready for a ride, gal?" he asked, reaching for her mane.

That was when an arm looped around his throat.

Chapter Eleven

Davy Crockett reacted automatically. Gripping the sinewy arm with his free hand, he bent at the waist and heaved. His attacker sailed up and over his shoulder, landing with a grunt a few feet away. Taking a bound, Davy hiked Liz. An upturned, frightened face gave him momentary pause.

It was a boy. Barely fifteen, if he was a day. Desperately, he clawed at a knife on his hip, but it was as if the hilt were smeared with grease. In his panic, he could not seem to grab it.

Liz swished down. The stock caught the youth across the head and left him as senseless as a tree stump.

Where there was one, there were bound to be more. Davy entwined his fingers in the mare's mane and vaulted astride her back. She pranced nervously, calming when he patted her neck and spoke softly. By tugging on the mane and slapping her sides with his legs, Davy prodded her into a trot.

Off in the night, someone hollered. Another, closer, took up the refrain, and soon half a dozen voices were raised in alarm. Davy heard but did not see an arrow buzz past his head. Pointing Liz at the sky, he thumbed back the hammer and fired, uttering a Comanche war whoop for good measure. His aim was to give the herd a case of the jitters, to cause them to mill about and keep the guards from getting a bead on him. But that single shot had a much greater effect, one he did not foresee.

The herd stampeded. He sensed a swell of motion, listened to the drum of countless hooves growing louder by the second. Harsh whinnies, unending nickers, blended in a rising tide as the enormous herd gathered momentum.

Davy was on the north edge of the herd. By rights, the animals should have stampeded to the south, *away* from the sound of the shot. That was the logical thing for them to do. But there is no logic to blind fear. Fear cripples the mind. When under its sway, even the most rational of creatures becomes like a terrified rabbit, running wildly wherever whim dictates. In this instance, the herd surged *toward* Davy.

The mare flew along with her head low. Davy saw dark shapes dart in front of her, heard others pass to the rear. To the right a dark wave was cresting, sweeping across the plain. It churned and seethed like a living thing. Unless he got in the clear, he would be trampled under that flood of horseflesh.

Somewhere, a Comanche screamed. Others were yelling and whooping, striving in vain to stop an irresistible force.

A large black horse flashed by in front, so near that the mare had to veer to avoid a collision. Another animal struck her hindquarters. Jolted, Davy clung on, tucking Liz under his arm to keep from dropping it.

Another forty feet they raced. Thunder boomed and crackled, the cacophony of hooves like the rumble of an earthquake. The air itself vibrated. Davy's ears pulsed to the beat.

His mouth had gone so dry that when he tried to swallow, his throat hurt.

Deep in that roiling mass an animal whinnied shrilly. A

thud, a crunch-crunch-crunch, and the whinnies were stilled.

Davy felt certain that he would share its fate. He could not see the east edge of the herd. More and more horses were going by, so many that a collision appeared inevitable. He tensed, wondering how much pain there would be, whether he would feel each bone crack and shatter or whether it would all be over so quickly that he would be spared some torment.

Suddenly the open prairie was before him. Davy did not slow, but he did look back. The herd blotted out the grass for as far as the eye could see. It was heading straight for the village, a tidal wave no one could withstand.

Comanches were running every which way. Mothers hustled children to the north or south. Warriors formed a line to attempt the impossible—to turn the herd before it destroyed all they held dear.

Davy frowned and almost turned the mare. He had not meant for this to happen. Despite everything, he had no hankering to bring wholesale destruction down on the tribe.

A few of the warriors waved burning brands. Others flapped blankets or robes. Bravely, they planted themselves in the herd's path. Some succeeded in parting the seething wave; others did not. Those who failed were buried, their screams snuffed by the clamor. A lodge crumpled, then another. A woman shrieked.

Davy did not watch the rest. Making for the hills, he soon wound among them to the spring. As he rode up, he was bewildered to find everyone else gone. "They left without me?" he said aloud.

"No."

Flavius strode out of the shadows and grasped the Irishman's leg. "You're a sight for sore eyes, ol' coon," he declared. On hearing the horse approach, he had taken cover with the Texians. Better safe than sorry, as the old saw went. "We thought you might be a Comanche."

149

"They'll have their hands full for quite a spell," Davy said. "It's safe for us to light a shuck."

Farley Tanner, his sister, and the men from San Antonio stepped from the darkness. "I wish to hell we could," the tall Texian said angrily.

"What's wrong?"

Flavius explained, concluding with "Kerr can't have much of a start. A couple of hours, we reckon. Find us some Indian ponies of our own, and in the morning we'll take out after him."

"It's not that simple." Davy had not dismounted, and now he turned the mare to the south. "The Comanche herd is scattered from here to Canada. We'd need a whole day, maybe two, to round up enough animals. And with the Comanches out rustling them up too, we'd have the devil to pay to do it without more bloodshed."

"So what do you propose?" Taylor asked.

"I'll go after Kerr and fetch your own horses back."

Anxiety ripped at Flavius's innards, just as it did every time they were separated. One of these times, he dreaded, they would not be reunited, leaving him stranded. "I don't know," he hedged. "That Kerr is a mean cuss. Wouldn't it be smarter to take at least one of us along? I could ride double."

"No." Davy had decided what needed doing. "We'd never catch him that way." He touched his coonskin cap. "Keep your hair on, gents, and lay low until I return."

Taylor stepped in front of the mare. "One thing, Crockett. You're under no obligation to bring Kerr back alive. After what he's done, none of us will hold it against you if you put windows in his skull." He stepped aside. "I just wanted to put your conscience at rest."

Davy clucked to the mare.

"Be careful, hoss," Farley called out. "He's as tricky as he is sidewinder mean. Watch his right boot. He keeps a dagger hid there."

Waving, Davy galloped off. The stricken look Flavius gave him was like that of a child deathly afraid of being deserted. He smiled encouragement, but the mullygrubs had Flavius in their grip again. No one could sulk and pout like Flavius Harris.

The mare settled into a mile-eating gait, and for three solid hours he pushed her southward. Thereafter, ten minutes out of every sixty he dismounted and walked. Weariness dulled him, but he shrugged off each bout.

A pink tinge to the east heralded a crisp dawn. Davy scouted for tracks, roaming half a mile to either side. Finding none, he looped wide to the east, then to the west, then back again, swinging in wider circles. Pricking him was the worry that Kerr had not headed for Texas, but was bound for St. Louis instead. He'd never catch up.

The sun had climbed an hour into the blue vault when Davy came over a knoll, spooking quail into fluttery flight. One ran off, and as his gaze followed it, he beheld churned earth. Electrified, he examined the spot closely.

Four horses, moving at a rapid walk, had gone by within the past hour. *Shod* horses.

"Got you."

Forking the mare, the Tennessean gave chase. There was no more rest for his tired mount, no more walking her to conserve her energy. Davy spurred her on when she flagged. He showed no compassion when she balked. Too much was at stake; too many lives hinged on the outcome.

Shortly before noon he came on fresh droppings. Shortly after noon he was surprised to spy a thin, smoky tendril. Had Kerr stopped for a meal? Davy would have bet the few coins in his poke that the Texian would not halt until evening.

In a convenient gulch he hid the mare. He did not like leaving her untied, but he did not have a rope. He counted on her being so winded that she would not stray off while he was gone.

The smoke was a mile off. A mile across essentially flat,

151

open terrain. Mostly he was on his hands and knees, rising into a crouch when the grass was high enough to screen him.

Kerr had chosen well. A hollow half an acre was bordered by a steep, bare bank on the west side. In its shade were tethered the four horses. Seated at the fire were Heather and Becky, their backs to the north rim. Of Kerr there was no sign.

Davy did not like it. Where had the Texian gone? Hunting? Heeding Nature's call? He scoured the hollow, then the prairie beyond.

Heather shifted and began to turn her head. Rising up onto his knees, Davy waved to attract her attention, but she did not twist all the way around and did not spot him. He assumed Kerr had bound both or else they would have jumped on a horse and skedaddled. As the minutes dragged and the Texian did not appear, Davy grew impatient. He might be able to sneak on down there, untie mother and daughter, and get the hell out before Kerr came back.

Gliding along the crest to a grassy slope, Davy descended. Liz was cocked and firmly against his shoulder. Hugging the base, he jogged to the camp. The horses showed little interest. They were as weary as the mare. He stalked past them until he could see Heather and Becky plainly.

They could also see him. Kerr had trussed them something awful, binding their ankles, their wrists, and their arms to their sides. In addition, they had been gagged with strips from Heather's dress.

"Hold on," Davy said. "I'll have you free in two shakes of a lamb's tail."

Heather's eyes were as wide as saucers. Vigorously shaking her head, she mouthed incoherent words. Becky whined like a lost puppy and jiggled wildly. Sheer excitement, Davy reckoned as he sank onto a knee next to the girl and dropped a hand to his tomahawk.

A metallic click turned the Tennessean to stone. Gruff laughter spilled from behind him, and a voice as cold as arctic wind stated flatly, "Don't so much as twitch, coonskin, or those females will be wearin' your brains."

Davy did as he was directed. Out of the corner of an eye he saw part of the bank on the other side of the horses dissolve. The Texian had scooped out a depression big enough to lie in and covered himself with the loose dirt. A damned clever trick, worthy of Davy himself.

Kerr sidled around, his rifle level. "I had me a hunch at least one of you would be on my tail," he said, sneering. "I guessed it would be Taylor. That son of a bitch never has cottoned to me. But it don't hardly matter. You're going to be just as dead as he would be."

Experience had taught Davy that nine times out of ten a man could talk himself out of a tight scrape. Tavern drunks, barroom bullies, ruffians, and cutthroats, he'd encountered them all at one time or another, and in most cases he had been able to fend off a beating, or worse. It didn't *always* work, but it was better than the alternative. Adopting a carefree air, he grinned at the unkempt Texian. "Go ahead. Shoot me."

"Let me get this straight. You *want* me to give you a new nostril?"

Davy nodded. "The others are close by. They're bound to hear and come on the run. You won't get a hundred yards, you miserable polecat."

Kerr stiffened, surveying the skyline. "You're bluffin', Tennessee. You're alone." Shifting, he hunkered to make a smaller target of himself. "If the others were with you, they'd be here."

"Oh, they're out there, all right," Davy said glibly. "They have the hollow covered in case you make a break for it." Enjoying the doubt he had inspired, Davy nonchalantly leaned back. "But don't take my word for it. Show yourself. Climb that slope and raise your head up. Then we'll see whose brains get splattered."

"You're lyin' through your teeth," Kerr spat, but he

lacked conviction. Licking his lips, he glanced over a shoulder, then caught himself and glared at the Irishman. "I always pegged you for a sneaky bastard."

Davy sighed. "Be that as it may, there's only one way for you to leave this hollow alive."

"What might that be?"

"Mount your horse and ride out. I made Taylor promise not to kill you if Mrs. Dugan and Becky were unharmed."

"Why would you do that for me?"

"I did it for them." Davy nodded at Heather and Becky. "I won't chance either of them being hit in the cross fire, or for you to kill them to spite us. Let them live and you live. It's as simple as that."

"Taylor and Farley and Ormbach agreed?"

"Why not? They're as mad as wet hens, naturally. But they're not out for blood. And now that Farley has Marcy safe, the only thing he wants is to get her home to San Antonio."

"You found her?"

"And stole a bunch of Comanche horses, to boot. That's how we caught up with you so soon."

It sounded plausible. As Davy's own pa had once said after Davy talked himself out of a licking for having neglected his chores, he "could be as slick as axle grease" when the need arose. Davy congratulated himself and exaggerated a yawn. "What'll it be? I don't have all day."

Kerr was in a stew. Scanning the rim, he constantly swiveled. "I think you're pullin' my leg," he said at last. "And there's a way to prove it." Rising, he jammed the muzzle of his rifle against Davy's neck. "Throw down that pistol and that hatchet."

So much for the benefit of a glib tongue. Davy obeyed, and was roughly hauled erect. Smiling as if he did not have a care in the world, he commented, "I guess Taylor was right. He claimed that you wouldn't believe me. He said you were too dumb to know when you were well off."

"Taylor said that?" Kerr snarled, and shook Davy as a terrier might a rat. "Too bad they didn't send him down instead of you. I'd gut that bastard just for the thrill of it, and make him choke on his own intestines."

"You can still make a liar of him. Mount up and leave."

Kerr let go and stepped back. Indecision twisted his bearish features. He was on the verge of giving in; Davy just knew it. To prod him, Davy said, "If you're worried about being shot, take me along as a hostage. They're not about to let anything happen to the Dugans or me."

"No, they're not, are they?" Kerr's mouth quirked upward. "That means I hold all the aces, don't I?"

Davy did not like the sound of that, or Kerr's gleeful expression. "I wouldn't push my luck if I were you."

Growling deep in his throat, the Texian took a step and rammed his rifle against Heather's bosom. "Do you hear me out there?" he bellowed. "Taylor? Farley? I've got my gun lined up with this woman's heart. Either waltz on down with your hands in the air, or so help me, the little girl gets to see her ma die!"

"No!" Davy exclaimed, and coiled to lunge.

"Don't you!" Kerr warned. Eyes ablaze, as feral as a cornered wolf, he gouged the barrel in deeper. Heather grimaced and tried to pull away, but being bound severely hampered her movements.

"Don't hurt her," Davy begged.

"Shut your mouth, Crockett." Glancing at the east crest, Kerr hollered, "Taylor! I know you can hear me! I'll give you until the count of five!" He paused. "One!"

Davy was at his wit's end. Unless he did something, on account of his bluff the woman was going to die.

"Two!"

Confessing the ruse might result in his own death, but Davy saw no other way out.

"Three!"

"I lied."

"What?" Kerr was so intent on the top of the hollow that he was not paying much attention.

"You were right all along. I came alone."

"I don't believe you." Kerr jumped when one of the horses stamped a foot. "Four!" he roared. As tightly strung as a fiddle string, he was primed to shoot anyone or anything that gave him any excuse.

Davy was fit to be tied. The Texian wouldn't believe the truth, but did believe his lies. What was he to do?

Far to the north, Flavius Harris faced a different dilemma. What was he to do if Davy never returned? Venturing to the Mississippi by his lonesome was a daunting notion. He'd soon wrestle a grizzly.

Dawn had broken chill and stark. Lacking blankets, unable to build a fire for fear of its being spotted by the Comanches, he had spent a thoroughly miserable night, tossing fitfully, waking frequently. Tired and hungry, Flavius rubbed his empty stomach and wondered how the soles of his boots would taste.

The Texians huddled together most of the morning. In spite of the setbacks they had suffered, they were in remarkably fine spirits. Rescuing Marcella Tanner had a lot to do with it. They were terribly upset, though, at being unable to save the other woman, and at one point Flavius overheard them discussing how they might yet do so.

Ironically, Farley's sister was the one who talked them out of it. "I appreciate how you feel," she told them, "but you'd only throw your lives away. She hasn't been right in the head since we were taken. For days all she would do was babble and cry. It got so I fretted the Comanches would kill her."

"That happens, I hear," Taylor said. "But if we took her back—"

"She wouldn't go," Marcy said. "Trust me. We talked about it every day. She was content there. Why, once she even vowed that she would rather die than leave."

Taylor dismissed the declaration with a wave. "The poor woman is horribly confused. She doesn't know what she wants."

Marcy would not be denied. "Farley, I expect you to believe me. Try to snatch her and none of you will escape alive. Fortune smiled on you once. Please don't push your luck."

Amen, Flavius thought. It pleased him no end when, after a long debate, the three men relented. They agreed to tell the other woman's kin she was dead. "It's best all around," Marcy concluded.

Now it was past noon, and Flavius was hungrier than ever. The Texians lounged near the spring, Marcy's head on her brother's arm. She had unwound her braids so her hair cascaded over her shoulders and had ripped beads from her buckskin dress, doing what she could to remove the stamp of the Comanches on her person and her attire.

Restless, Flavius walked to the nearest hill and climbed. He had no particular destination, no goal other than to stretch his legs.

Sitting still for any length of time was difficult. Anyone burdened by as many worries as he had was bound to be all het up.

The hills had been quiet since Davy departed. Flavius gathered that the Comanches were busy rounding up their stock and salvaging their effects. It should keep them busy for days, until long after Davy came back.

At the summit, Flavius inhaled and stretched. He saw the spring and the Texians, saw a number of antelope to the east, a hawk to the north. Continuing to turn, he glimpsed clusters of grazing horses scattered from the stream to the horizon. His initial estimate had been wrong. Collecting every last one would take a month of Sundays.

A lot of activity was taking place at the village, but Flavius could not distinguish details. Warriors on horseback were in the vicinity of the stream. Others, on foot, were spread among the cottonwoods. Hunting runaways, Flavius reasoned.

Then seven or eight Comanches left the trees and spread out. They had their heads bent low, and every now and again one dipped to the ground to inspect it. A pinprick of apprehension stuck Flavius, expanding into a sword of raw alarm when one of the warriors rose and pointed at the hills.

Another raised an arm toward the cottonwoods. Half a dozen riders promptly trotted into the open, listened to whatever the man was saying, and quirted their mounts into a trot.

Flavius's scalp itched as he spun on a heel and dashed down the incline. The Comanches must be thirsting for revenge. They still had plenty of horses to round up, yet they were out hunting those responsible for last night's disaster.

Ormbach was the only one not dozing when Flavius puffed to a stop. "On your feet!" he bawled. "The Indians are heading this way."

Farley sprang erect, pulling his sister up with him. But Taylor only rose onto an elbow and arched an eyebrow. "Are you sure? Maybe it's a hunting party."

"Lie there if you want," Flavius snapped, "but they're going to be on us like ducks on a bunch of june bugs if we don't light a rag for the high grass." As an afterthought, he said, "I have a hunch they're tracking the mare Davy stole."

"Damn." Farley moved swiftly eastward. "If it ain't chickens, it's feathers." He smacked one of his fancy pistols, informing Marcy, "I won't let them get their filthy hands on you again, sis. I'd rather we both died."

Ormbach hustled after them, as did Flavius, but Taylor dragged his heels. "Maybe we should stick close to the spring. Without water we won't last long."

"And give them the advantage of the high ground?" Farley responded. "Why not slit your wrists and save them the trouble?" He shook his head. "Me, I'm not anxious to take the big jump yet. When I go down, it'll be under a heap of red devils.''

Ormbach was checking his rifle. ''That goes double for me. Harp lessons don't interest me nohow.''

''What are we standing around for, then?'' Marcy demanded.

They ran. For a while Flavius forgot about his empty stomach and his sore muscles and the shave he needed. It was amazing how a little thing like being in mortal jeopardy helped a person's perspective.

Taylor passed him as they wound along the bottom of the last hill. Flavius did not like being at the rear and hurried to overtake the Texian, but a sharp pain in his right sole thwarted him. A small stone had somehow slid into his boot.

Stopping, Flavius sat and tugged at the offending footwear. Running had made him sweaty. He had made a mistake by not helping himself to a final drink from the spring before they left. It might be days before he enjoyed another.

The darn boot refused to cooperate. It fought him every inch, the damp leather clinging to him like a second skin. Matilda had made it, as she did all his clothes, and she had a habit of fashioning everything a mite too tight. Wishful thinking on her part, he reckoned.

Flavius had to yank and twist to get it off. Upending it, he watched the stone tumble. His toes were sore, so he briefly massaged them, relishing the sensation. As he slid them back in, he glanced toward the plain and saw the Texians a good distance off. No one had realized he had fallen behind. He was all set to yell when the clatter of another stone whipped him around.

Something—or someone—was back there.

Chapter Twelve

It was a ruse as old as the emerald hills of Tennessee. A trick no one would use except as a last resort. And it was the only ploy Davy Crockett could think of. Glancing past Kerr, he pretended to be startled by what he saw and exclaimed, "Don't shoot, Taylor! We can still talk this out!"

Most men would have recognized the bluff for what it was. But Kerr was in the grip of blind blood lust. In his highstrung state he was not thinking straight. Flinging Heather from him, he whirled, bringing the rifle to his shoulder.

Davy pounced. Hooking a foot around the Texian's legs, he hurtled forward, tripping Kerr. They both went down, Davy on top. He grabbed for the rifle but missed. Kerr was as slippery as an eel. Twisting, he backhanded Davy across the face, then sought to shove the rifle against Davy's chest and squeeze the trigger.

Swatting the barrel aside, Davy lunged and wrapped both hands around the gun. They fought to gain sole possession, rolling back and forth as they heaved and pulled and twisted.

Davy won, but when he elevated the stock to bash Kerr over the head, agony exploded in his groin. The Texian had kneed him.

A muffled scream rang out. Steel flashed in the sunlight. Davy threw himself backward, felt burning in his shoulder. Scrambling upright, he saw a tear in his hunting shirt where the blade had nicked him.

Kerr was a skilled knife fighter. He came in swiftly, in a crouch, the weapon held low down, the knife positioned to slash or thrust.

Davy backpedaled to gain room. He evaded a cut, leaped clear of a blow aimed at his throat. Suddenly Kerr rushed him, delivering a flurry that drove Davy to the rear. A crafty smirk lit the Texian's face. The reason became apparent when Davy backed into the dirt wall.

"You've got no place to go now, Tennessee," Kerr gloated. "When I'm through with you, you'll be in tiny pieces."

It gave Davy a moment to set himself. When the Texian lanced the blade at his heart, he pivoted, caught hold of Kerr's wrist, and levered Kerr forward, simultaneously thrusting out a foot. Kerr smashed into the wall, but recovered instantly. Bellowing like an irate bear, he tried to tear his wrist free. Failing at that, he kicked at Davy's groin again.

The Irishman learned from his mistakes. He was ready, and by shifting his hip, he took the brunt of the kick on his thigh instead of where it would hurt the most.

To give Kerr a taste of his own medicine, Davy pumped his knee high up between the Texian's legs. Kerr grunted, then gurgled and turned scarlet. His grip weakened. Davy took advantage and reached for the knife to disarm his enemy, but the man had plenty of fight left in him. Kerr drove his forehead forward into Davy's face.

Stars exploded before Davy's eyes. Jolted, dazed, he staggered, half afraid his nose had been broken. He had lost his hold on Kerr, and he groped wildly for another. A second muted scream warned him that the Texian was closing in again.

Blinking and shaking his head, Davy cleared it just as cold steel swept at his jugular. He threw himself to the left, rolled, and rose on one knee. Groping for dirt to throw in Kerr's face, he found something better. His fingers closed on the handle of his tomahawk.

The Texian charged. Davy met him head-on. Metal rasped against metal. He parried a rapier thrust, countered, but did not score. Circling one another, they each sought an opening. Kerr thought he saw one and stabbed the knife at Davy's midsection. Countering, Davy cleaved the tomahawk at the Texian's cheek. The blow was blocked.

They joined in earnest, weaving a tapestry of flashing steel. Circling and striking and blocking, they were a whirl-wind of motion. Evenly matched, they traded blows until both of them were breathing heavily.

Kerr unexpectedly jumped to one side, out of range. "You're tougher than I figured, coonskin," he said begrudg-ingly. "Tell you what. We'll end it. Let me take my horse and go. No blood spilled. No hard feelings. What do you say?"

Davy lowered the tomahawk a fraction, pondering. In that moment of vulnerability, the Texian struck. Kerr's arm was invisible, the knife flying from his fingers like a bolt out of the blue. Davy had no time to duck or dodge. He had been caught flat-footed. In sheer reflex he brought the tomahawk up, and quite by accident the blade clanged against its head instead of sinking into his flesh. Deflected, the knife clattered to he ground.

"Damn your bones!"

Kerr barreled forward, batting the tomahawk to the left. He wrapped both brawny hands around Davy's neck. Thick fingers gouged in deep. Davy couldn't breathe. He was bowled over, the Texian landing astride his chest.

"I've got you now!"

Davy, sputtering, tried to bury the tomahawk in Kerr's side. But Kerr was too canny for him. Clamping a knee onto Davy's right arm, the Texian pinned it. And all the while those iron fingers dug in deeper, ever deeper. Davy tore at them with his left hand, but it was like trying to peel metal bars apart.

"Die!" Kerr raged. "Die!"

Davy just might. Already his lungs ached and a gray veil fogged his vision. He bucked upward, but Kerr outweighed him by a good sixty pounds. He wrenched sideways, but the Texian stayed on. And those fingers gouged in farther.

I'm being strangled, Davy thought. It was strange, but his mind was in a detached state, almost as if he were another person watching the struggle from a little ways off. He saw himself weaken, saw Kerr's gleam of triumph.

Then a new figure tumbled into the scene. It was Heather curled into a ball, rolling like a giant tumbleweed. She slammed into the Texian, throwing him off balance, and although trussed up, she rammed her feet into his spine. Kerr was sent sprawling.

Suddenly Davy was no longer detached from his own body. Aflame with pain, gasping for air, he pushed to his feet. Dimly, he was aware that he still held the tomahawk. He saw Kerr rush him like an enraged bull, and he brought the tomahawk crashing down. In his befuddled frame of mind, he landed a glancing blow, not a fatal one.

Struck on the temple, Kerr tottered to one side, clutching himself. Blood smeared his fingers when he lowered his hand, exposing a nasty gash. "You son of a bitch!" he roared. Then he did what neither of them had, oddly enough, considered doing until that moment. He stabbed a hand at one of the flintlocks tucked under his belt.

Davy let go of the tomahawk and did the same. He was a shade too slow. Kerr's pistol cleared first. The muzzle

164

belched lead and smoke. Not feeling an impact, Davy answered in kind.

The Texian was thrown backward. A red stain marked his shoulder. Swaying on his feet, he grabbed for his second flintlock.

This time Davy was faster. His pistol cracked, spitting flame. A heavy mallet seemed to slam into Kerr, catapulting him to the dirt in a disjointed heap. He struggled to rise, gasped once, and keeled over, limp.

Sore and bruised and bleeding from the knife wound, Davy slowly lowered both flintlocks. Every muscle hurt. His head throbbed. Turning, he confirmed that Heather and Becky were all right. Neither had caught a stray ball.

Somehow, Heather had worked her gag loose. "You did it!" she breathed. "I was so worried there for a minute."

"Makes two of us," Davy quipped. Sinking to his knees beside her, he set down the pistols and bent over the knots on her wrists. "Give me a bit. I'm a little shaky yet."

"Look out!"

Her cry came too late. Hands clamped onto Davy's neck from behind. He was pushed forward, almost onto his face. Only by throwing both hands flat was he able to save himself. It felt as if his neck was being crushed. A knee connected with his backbone, spiking exquisite torment the length of his body.

Davy surged upward and threw all his weight into a turn, even as he swung his arm up and around. It worked. Free of the Texian's grasp, he raised his fists to defend himself, marveling at the apparition that confronted him.

Kerr was pale and caked with perspiration. A wide red stain covered the front of his buckskins, from shoulder to waist. Yet there he stood, grimly glaring, like a vicious alley cat about to spring.

What does it take to kill a Texian? Davy wondered. He'd heard tales, saloon gossip, that Texians were a notoriously hardy bunch. They were supposed to eat nails for breakfast, anvils for supper.

A fist rocked Davy on his heels, another sent him tottering. Planting both legs, he braced for another onslaught. Kerr waded in, throwing punches right and left, seeking by sheer force of will to batter Davy down. Davy gave as good as he got. One of Kerr's blows crunched his teeth together. One of his set Kerr's eyelids to fluttering.

Growling like a mad dog, the Texian lowered his head and hurtled forward. Davy's breath whooshed from his lungs as the human battering ram folded him at the waist. Locked in combat, they pitched onto the ground.

Once again Kerr wrapped his hands around Davy's throat. His features contorted in savage exultation, Kerr squeezed harder than ever, spittle frothing his lips. "This time!" he hissed. "This time you're mine!"

Davy raked an open palm across the Texian's face. The nose broke with a sharp snap, the upper lip was pulped. But Kerr did not relent. The pressure on Davy's neck was beyond belief. In desperation he boxed Kerr's ears. When that produced no result, he dug his thumbs into the Texian's eyes.

Howling, Kerr scuttled backward, tears gushing over his cheeks. As luck would have it, his hand brushed his rifle. Blinking to clear his vision, he snatched the gun up and brought it to bear.

Davy was halfway to his feet. Taking an awkward leap, he tackled the Texian. The barrel smacked his head, and he flung out an elbow to brush it away. Without warning, the rifle discharged in his ear. He heard Heather call Becky's name. Fearing the girl had been hit, he risked a glance, and paid for his mistake by suffering a blow to the jaw that left him flat on his back, his senses spinning.

A vengeful fury in human form heaved above him. Kerr posed with the stock ready to crash down. With no conscious thought on his part, Davy lashed out with both legs, bashing the Texian's shins. Kerr swore luridly as he was brought down in a tangle of limbs and rifle.

Davy was winded, an ache in his side hurting abominably. Sluggishly, he rose, his only consolation the fact that Kerr was hurt worse and took longer to get up. Across a span of three feet they faced each other, seething hatred evident in the Texian's dark eyes. It was that inferno of hatred, Davy mused, that gave Kerr the inhuman strength to keep going.

Kerr had dropped the rifle, lost his knife. His shirt was soaked red, his face in ruins. Yet he straightened and clenched his fists to continue their clash.

In all his born days, Davy had never seen the like. If all Texians were as indestructible as Kerr, they would be unbeatable in battle. A small band of them could hold off an entire army. An army of Texians would be invincible.

Kerr stepped to the right, wary, tense, teeth bared. He flicked a jab, delivered an uppercut that missed, and followed through with a looping left. Davy warded them off. Throwing up an arm when Kerr threw a cross, Davy was taken aback when the Texian dived past him. The cross had been a feint. Kerr had seen something lying on the grass.

It was Davy's tomahawk. Venting a feral growl, the Texian arced it around, intending to sink it into Davy's chest. Only a mishap saved him. For as Davy skipped backward, his foot slipped and he fell. The tomahawk swept overhead, clipping his coonskin cap.

Kerr's breath husked raggedly. Setting himself, he brought the tomahawk down at Davy's skull. Davy jerked to the left. The blade thunked into the earth next to his ear, leaving Kerr bent low over him. For an instant their eyes locked and sparked.

Davy whipped his right foot into the Texian's sternum. Kerr staggered backward, grasping for support where there was none. Brought up short by colliding with the wall, he paused, marshaling his strength.

Anxious to see about Becky, Davy rolled and rose. As he

did, he saw Kerr's knife within reach. Palming it, he reversed his grip, holding it by the tip of the blade. As a boy he had practiced throwing knives to where he could hit a knothole the size of a walnut nine times out of ten at a distance of ten paces. As an adult he rarely practiced, but some skills stayed with a man, becoming second nature. He put it to the test the very next second.

Kerr raised the tomahawk and charged one more time, his face as red as his shirt, his chest heaving from the monumental exertion. He was on his last legs, and they both knew it. Every iota of energy he had left, every bit of strength and stamina, he put into this final effort.

The knife met the Texian midway. Steel and flesh joined. Kerr grunted and stopped dead, as if he had run into a brick wall. He glared at the hilt jutting from his body, then glared at Davy, his hatred undiminished even in this, his last few moments of life. His mouth opened, but whatever he wanted to say was left unspoken. Gagging, he folded at the knees. Wheezing, he pitched forward. His body went into convulsions. His tongue protruded. True to his nature, he twisted his neck to gaze balefully at Davy. He died radiating spite.

Davy could not say exactly why he shuddered. Turning, he saw Heather next to Becky, and ran over. Mother and daughter were propped against each other. In the ground next to the child's leg was a furrow that ended in a hole.

"I thought she had been hit," Heather said weakly.

Freeing them wasn't easy, even using the knife. Kerr had tied the ropes so tightly that Davy had to exercise extreme care not to cut them. As he finished with Becky, she flung her arms around him and sobbed.

"What about the body?" Heather asked at length.

"Buzzards and coyotes have to eat" was Davy's response. After gathering all the weapons, he reloaded the guns. The horses were already saddled. So once the fire had been stamped out, they mounted and rode north. Davy remembered to claim the mare.

The Dugans were uncommonly quiet. Given their ordeal, Davy did not blame them. In light of the shape they were in, he was reluctant to push very hard. By nightfall they had covered half as many miles as he could have done alone.

Camp was made in a gully. An obliging rabbit was the main ingredient in a hot stew. Stars speckled the firmament when Davy spread out blankets for each of them and took a seat on his. Becky, who had not uttered a word in hours, gave him a probing stare and cleared her throat.

"Can you tell me why, Mr. Crockett?"

"Why what?"

"Why are there wicked people like Mr. Kerr? Why does God let bad men do bad things to us? Why do we have to suffer?"

Davy chuckled. "Lordy, girl. If I could answer that, I'd be the wisest person who ever lived. Truth is, no two people can agree on the reason. Some say the Devil is to blame, and give him credit for all the things that go wrong. Some think the evil men do takes root in their own hearts. Others believe bad things just happen."

"It's not right. No one should ever have to hurt."

What could Davy say? How could he get it across that pain and suffering were part and parcel of life? That from the cradle to the grave most folks engaged in one long effort to ward it off, to make their lives as bearable, as pleasant, as possible? His grandma once told him that without pain there could be no pleasure, for the only way to appreciate the latter was to have tasted the former. A bizarre notion, yet it made warped sense.

He stayed awake until midnight, dozed fitfully for a bit, and slumbered heavily once he stopped resisting. Breakfast consisted of leftover stew and—wonder of wonders—coffee found in Kerr's saddlebags.

Davy felt like a new man when they started out. Heather chattered about the rich social life of St. Louis, while Becky hummed or sang. No one would guess that they were hundreds of miles from the nearest outpost of civilization, three pieces of driftwood afloat in an endless green sea.

By the middle of the afternoon Davy spied the hills. Reining up, he rose in the stirrups to scour the plain to the west of them. No Comanches were evident, but he had a powerful feeling Two Claws and company were still in the vicinity. "I want the two of you to wait right here."

"Shouldn't we stay together?" Heather responded uneasily.

"I can get in and out quicker alone." Davy did not elaborate on why that might be necessary. Giving her the lead rope, he trotted to the flank of the hill situated farthest to the southeast. Winding in among them, he drew rein when close enough to the spring to overhear conversation—had there been any. An eerie stillness hung heavy over the land.

Dismounting, Davy advanced on foot. The spring was tranquil, its surface shimmering with sunshine. Flavius and the Texians were gone, and there was no sign they had been there in days. Charred coals were all that was left of the fire.

Tracks there were plenty of. Moccasin tracks crisscrossed the area, many more than a few hunters would have made. The conclusion was obvious: The Comanches had been searching for his friends.

Running to the horse, Davy swung onto the saddle and commenced a search of his own. So jumbled were the prints that it took more than an hour for him to sort out which direction Flavius and the rest had gone. To the east. But after traveling almost to the open prairie, he was baffled to find that the tracks vanished into thin air.

He had to rove back and forth for a quarter of an hour before he solved the mystery. Tiny telltale brush marks were the key. Someone, evidently using a shirt or other garment, had wiped out every boot print from that point on.

Davy had to go well out onto the plain to pick up the trail again. The fugitives had fled to the southeast. There was nothing to indicate the Comanches had gone after them, but it wouldn't do to take anything for granted. Marking the spot by tearing out a wide circle of grass, he returned to Heather and Becky.

The mother was pacing nervously. Davy explained, then led the pair to the spot, and from there they hurried after Flavius and the others. Soon the tracks adopted a southerly bearing, as they would if the Texians were heading home.

Nightfall caught them in the open. Davy allowed a small fire but shielded it with their saddles. Eager to be off, he was up before sunrise. Heather grumbled and Becky was as slow as molasses, but presently they were under way.

Noon came and went. It was the middle of the afternoon when Davy set eyes on a sight that chilled his blood. A large flock of vultures circled ahead. "Stay here," he told his companions.

"Not on your life," Heather replied.

Davy did not deem it wise to expose Becky to a possible slaughter, but he did not make an issue of it. His fears proved groundless. Instead of bloated human corpses, the buzzards had been attracted by the fresh carcass of a bull buffalo. An old bull, an outcast that had been wandering alone. Scavengers had been at the haunches and hind end, but they had not obliterated cut marks made by several big knives.

"Flavius and the others?" Becky asked.

"They ate and pushed on," Davy confirmed.

An hour and a half later, as Davy skirted a knoll, the sorrel pricked its ears and nickered. Galloping on around, he spied figures running off. "Wait!" he hollered, just as a rifle cracked and a ball zinged past his cheek.

Flavius Harris lowered Matilda and grinned like a boy who had just been granted his fondest birthday wish. "Davy!" he exclaimed, bursting for joy inside. "It's really you!" He ran to greet his friend, choosing to forget for the moment that he had nearly killed him. Frayed nerves were to blame, thanks to little sleep and the ever-present threat of being discovered by the Comanches.

Heather reined up alonside Davy and scanned the grass. She beamed when Farley Tanner appeared. If there was any doubt as to how close they had grown, it was dispelled by the passionate embrace they shared.

Taylor clasped the Irishman's hand warmly. "Kerr?"

Davy shook his head.

"Too bad. He was never one to walk the straight and narrow, but I never figured he'd go as far as he did." The older Texian sighed. "I can't help feeling partly to blame. He'd still be alive if we hadn't asked him to come along."

"If a man is meant to drown, he'll drown in a desert."

Flavius gave his partner a hug, then smacked Davy's broad back. "It's over at last! Now we can light a shuck for the Mississippi. We'll go to where we cached our canoes and make for St. Louis. Another month or so, it's on to Tennessee. Elizabeth and Matilda will be tickled to see us. Why, I reckon—"

"Don't get ahead of yourself," Davy interrupted. Breaking the bad news did not sit well with him. "We can't head for the Mississippi just yet."

A terrible sensation washed over Flavius, like that he had when he nearly drowned in Baxter's Creek back home. "Why in blazes can't we?" he squeaked.

"There aren't enough horses to go around. Only five, and there are eight of us."

"So? We'll walk," Flavius said, knowing it was ridiculous but grasping at straws.

"Becky too?"

"Just one horse. That's all we need. Heather and her can ride double. The two of us will go on foot. It'll take us most of the summer, but we'll get there."

"No."

"God in heaven. Don't, Davy. Please."

"It's the right thing to do."

A lump formed in Flavius's throat and he bowed his head, overcome by grief so potent he could not bear it. Time after time his hopes had been raised. Time after time they had been dashed. He wanted to scream, to rant, to rail, to beat Davy senseless. Affection waged war with disappointment. Devotion battled despair. In the end, he said weakly, "What do you want to do?"

"Stay together, ride double, switch horses whenever one tires. That way none will go lame on us, and we can make good time." Davy put a hand on his friend's shoulder, but Flavius pulled away. "We'll help the Texians reach San Antonio safely, rest up a spell, then head for the States."

Taylor chimed in, saying, "Cheer up, friend. It will only take a week to ten days to get there. You'll love San Antonio. Everyone is right friendly. And you'll be the toast of the town for having helped rescue Marcy."

"I'd rather be home." Forlorn as could be, Flavius walked off to be by himself. But footsteps followed him, and he was denied the luxury.

"I'm sorry. Truly, deeply sorry."

"I know."

"If there were any other way, I'd do it."

"Quit making excuses. You have that damnable Crockett motto to live up to. But if you ask me, that damn saying is a curse. Mark my words. One of these days you'll rue the day your pa told it to you."

"Always be sure you're right, then go ahead." Davy stepped in front of Flavius and extended his hand. "Are we still friends?"

"Need you ask?" Flavius clasped it. "We don't always see eye to eye. I don't always agree with your highfalutin morals. But we've always been pards and we always will be."

Davy Crockett smiled. It was on to Texas. He would see new country, meet new people, have new experiences. Life was grand.

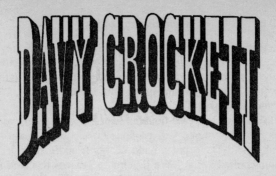

DAVY CROCKETT

Sioux Slaughter. With only his long rifle and his friend, Davy Crockett sets out, determined to see the legendary splendor of the Great Plains. But it may be one gallivant too many. He barely survives a mammoth buffalo stampede before he's ambushed—by a band of Sioux warriors with blood in their eyes.

___4157-X $3.99 US/$4.99 CAN

Homecoming. The Great Lakes territories are full of Indians both peaceful and bloodthirsty. And when the brave Davy Crockett and his friend save a Chippewa maiden from warriors of a rival tribe, their travels become a deadly struggle to save their scalps.

___4112-X $3.99 US/$4.99 CAN

Dorchester Publishing Co., Inc.
P.O. Box 6640
Wayne, PA 19087-8640

Please add $1.75 for shipping and handling for the first book and $.50 for each book thereafter. NY, NYC, and PA residents, please add appropriate sales tax. No cash, stamps, or C.O.D.s. All orders shipped within 6 weeks via postal service book rate. Canadian orders require $2.00 extra postage and must be paid in U.S. dollars through a U.S. banking facility.

Name_____
Address_____
City_____State_____Zip_____
I have enclosed $_____ in payment for the checked book(s).
Payment <u>must</u> accompany all orders. ☐ Please send a free catalog.

DAVY CROCKETT

BLOOD HUNT

David Thompson

With only his oldest friend and his trusty long rifle for company, Davy Crockett explores the wild frontier looking for adventure, and has the strength and cunning to face any enemy. But even he may have met his match when he gets caught between two warring tribes on one side and a dangerous band of white men on the other—all of them willing to die—and kill—for a group of stolen women. It is up to Crockett to save the women, his friend and his own hide if he wants to live to explore another day.

_4229-0 $3.99 US/$4.99 CAN

Dorchester Publishing Co., Inc.
P.O. Box 6640
Wayne, PA 19087-8640

Please add $1.75 for shipping and handling for the first book and $.50 for each book thereafter. NY, NYC, and PA residents, please add appropriate sales tax. No cash, stamps, or C.O.D.s. All orders shipped within 6 weeks via postal service book rate. Canadian orders require $2.00 extra postage and must be paid in U.S. dollars through a U.S. banking facility.

Name_____
Address_____
City_____State_____Zip_____
I have enclosed $_____ in payment for the checked book(s).
Payment <u>must</u> accompany all orders. ❑ Please send a free catalog.